SEED
of the
GODS

SEED
of the
GODS

LEAH SHRIFTER

Wild
ginger
Press

Seed of the Gods
© 2016 Susan L. Shrifter
www.leahshrifter.com

Printed in the USA
ISBN: 978-1-943190-07-2

Wild Ginger Press
www.wildgingerpress.com

For my younger self

Prologue

GENESIS, VI

1   *And it came to pass, when men began to multiply on the face
    of the earth and daughters were born unto them,*

2   *That the sons of God saw the daughters of men, that they were
    fair; and they took themselves wives of all whom they chose.*

4   *The giants were on the earth in those days; and also after
    that, when the sons of God came in unto the daughters of
    men and they bore children to them; these became the mighty
    men, who were of old the men of renown.*

"I tell you they are not Gods!"

The crowd of devoted worshippers gathered before the huge pillars of the vast stone Temple seemed to gasp together as one person. "Hush, foolish old man!" cried someone at the back. "You are so old you have gone silly, like a child. Gods, have mercy! He knows not what he says!"

The old man whipped about, his sparse gray hair and long beard floating in the breeze. He was taller than anyone else in the crowd and his clear blue eyes flashed the fire of youth as he sought out his would-be protector. He turned back and beseeched the people again.

"Look at them!" he shouted, extending his arms and pointing to the high Temple platform. "They are only bigger than we are! They threaten us with their fire-sticks and they take our food, our wine, and use our women for their selfish pleasure. They enslave us because we fear them and they force us to toil for them so they live in comfort and luxury. They are not Gods and they do not love us! They are big men, but far fewer than us. We can rise against them! They cannot fight us all, even with their fire-sticks."

"Get thee away from the blasphemer. Go now!" thundered A-Don, most powerful of all the Gods. His regal robe of purple and gold trim swirled about him as he strode from side to side above them on the platform. He spoke into the bottom of his metal speaking cup, which he held near his fiery orange hair and beard. The other giant Gods raised their fire-sticks, aiming into the frightened crowd.

As the God A-Don commanded, the people fled. They screamed and scattered like frightened chickens, grasping the hands of their children, dragging them away from the angry Gods. There would be none of the promised healings today for which all had assembled, happy to worship the Gods, their benevolent protectors. No, the Gods showed no mercy to those who defied them. The rebellious were swiftly punished, burned alive by the power of the

Gods' mighty weapons. No one wanted to hear the old man's agonized screams.

The God A-Don pointed his fire-stick at the lone figure below. The bright, hard metal of the fearsome weapon gleamed harshly in the noonday sun. Another God stepped forward, sneering at the defiant man, while others laughed in cruel amusement.

"Do what you will to me," shouted the old man, striding toward them. "We will not be your slaves forever!" He stopped in front of the platform and looked up, fixing his flashing eyes on each God in turn. He hawked and spat.

"You will die," pronounced A-Don. He thrust forth his mighty fire-stick and the killing fire spewed out at the old man. The brave rebel rooted his feet to the earth and riveted his eyes on the terrible flames. But before the fire could touch him, a sudden gust of wind blew it out as if it was only candlelight. The man's mouth fell open in silent wonder as the whirling wind enveloped him and swept him up into the blue summer skies. And then he was gone. The wind died as suddenly as it had come alive.

The Gods shouted their fury, unaware of a child staring up at them from the side of the Temple platform, the only one who had not fled with the rest of the people. She had seen the old man disappear and thus escape the wrath of the Gods. Turning, she stepped behind the high platform, unnoticed by the giants above her. She knew the old man had spoken the truth.

One

Sarai first heard the thoughts of the Gods in her eighth summer, on the morning of the day the brave old man defied the Gods. Yawning and stretching her hands above her into the morning sunlight, she sat up on her sleeping pallet in the back room where the few children slept who served the Gods in the Temple.

She had always slept there. One of the older priestesses, Melina, who guided her in her Temple duties, had explained that when Sarai was an infant, someone had left her on the Temple steps in a basket, covered only by a thin blanket, on a chilly winter morning. It was Melina who had discovered the wailing babe in the basket and taken her inside, fed her, clothed her and cared for her until she was old enough to begin work. Gentle, sorrowful Melina—whose thick, almond-colored coils of hair drooped in sympathy with her brown eyes reddened from weeping for the infant son she had lost only three days before—hugged the tiny girl to her swollen breasts and called her Sarai after her own mother, who had died several years ago. She nursed the babe with the milk that would have fed her son.

Melina and the other priestesses naturally assumed that someone with great love and respect for the Gods had gifted her Masters with her own child, to honor and serve them. Many people made gifts and sacrifices to the Gods; such a gift as little Sarai was not unusual, although most girls destined to become priestesses were hand-picked by the Gods themselves when they were older and coming into womanhood. Sarai was not likely to be chosen as a priestess, but would remain a servant in the Temple, living to do their bidding.

The sleepy child heard voices, men's voices, some laughing and some arguing crossly, so close they seemed to be inside her head. The Gods must be coming to the children's room to speak to them. But why? Sarai got up from under her scratchy, threadbare blanket. Her nimble fingers pulled her sleeping shift over her bare bottom as she quickly knelt in the servile position, her forehead resting on her sleeping pallet. "Wake up, get up!" she whispered loudly to the other sleeping children, peeking at them through her folded hands. "The Gods are here to speak to us!"

But no one woke, no one moved. Sarai raised her voice above a whisper, exhorting her companions to wake. But her efforts were fruitless. Only the dust moved in the morning sunbeams filtering through the cracks in the wall. The worried girl trembled, waiting. The Gods' raucous voices were loud in her ears, but they did not come. Cautiously, she sat up and looked through the edges of the rough hemp covering stretched across the entrance to the children's room. The Gods were not there outside, nor were they nearby. She could see no one, no man, woman, child or God outside the room.

In the suspended morning stillness, she again heard the Gods laughing and talking. She did not understand how she could hear them, but their voices continued. She sat, silent and unmoving, listening in wonder, her spirit hushed by this miracle of *hearing* that was with her.

Did you see that old hag yesterday, the ugly one with the warts all over her face and hands?

Oh yes, she was ugly all right! She brought that lamb stew especially for you, Jor-Gum. She's devoted to you—not that you deserve it. You should heal her today, get rid of those warts. Maybe some puny earth man would want her, then. I'll bet she's never had a man.

Jor-Gum scoffed, *So you think she's my special responsibility now? You heal her if you care that much! I just do the work I'm told to do.*

Loud, boisterous laughter and another God's voice. *We all do. That's why we're here, to carry out Home World's orders. We need to have some fun! Come on, Jor-Gum, give her a great healing! You're the one she adores. She'll sing your praises until she dies, which shouldn't be long from now. None of them live very long. Hah! Jor-Gum, the Adored One!* He guffawed until he coughed.

You know, I'm actually tired of all this worship and adoration, grumbled another *voice. I'm tired of these people—if you can really call them people. They aren't any bigger than the oxen. Not any smarter, either.*

Wouldn't do any good hitched up to a cart, volunteered one more before their laughter drowned out the rest of his words.

The poor child pressed her hands over her ears, desperate to shut out their mean, hurtful words. It did her no good. The big Gods' voices pounded inside her, beating her like clubs until she felt sick. She reached for her tunic, folded at the end of her sleeping pallet, pulled it over her and stumbled through the old hemp covering, ripping through it as if it were only a big cobweb. She stopped briefly to relieve herself in the commode area and then turned and vomited on top of her own waste. She washed hastily in the basin and then ran to find Melina. The Gods' loud, contemptuous voices continued in her head. No matter how hard she squeezed her fingers into her ears, she could not shut out their brutal words.

Sarai knew where to find her kind mentor. Melina was busy on the Temple platform, preparing many flower bouquets for the Healing Ceremony that would take place when the sun was high in the sky. As she had grown older, the Gods called less for her to worship them as a priestess and now she spent most of her days performing the same duties as the lowly Temple servants. At the back of the platform, Sarai scrambled up the ladder on bare feet.

"Melina, Melina!" She tugged at the priestess's long tunic. "Do you hear them? They're horrible! I can't get away from their voices!"

Melina carefully tucked the last white lily into the bouquet and turned to the crying girl she had grown to love as dearly as if she had been her own natural child. "Dear girl," she soothed, stroking Sarai's long black tresses, "what troubles you so? What voices do you hear?"

"You don't hear them?" Sarai's emerald-green eyes overflowed with tears.

"Hear who? No, I don't hear anyone but you, my love."

"It's them. It's the Gods! I hear them talking and they say horrible, cruel things about us—"

Shocked by the girl's unbelievable confession, Melina roughly covered her mouth so that Sarai could say no more. Seeing in the child's eyes that she knew to remain quiet, the frightened woman grabbed Sarai's arm and pulled her down the ladder into the gathering area. Their scurrying feet kicked up the dust of late summer as the older woman tugged the girl with her until they were far enough away from any who might hear them.

She spoke sternly to the wide-eyed child. "I don't know what you are hearing. I hope you only imagine it. It doesn't matter. Never speak of this again, not to me or to anyone."

"But—"

"Never! Never say another word to anyone, not even to me. You know how dangerous this is. Now I will not speak of it again. Come, child."

Sarai understood. She choked back the rest of her words, breathing hard, and wiped the tears from her face with the backs of her hands. She kissed Melina on the cheek and ran off to perform her own duties. She spoke not another word to anyone and worked without thinking, for the rough, cruel voices continued, overwhelming her, burying her own thoughts as if they were kicking dirt over them inside her head.

It was not until later that day, when the mad old man shouted to the crowd and spat his defiance at the Gods, that she found herself and her own will again. She watched him escape their wrath and listened the rest of the day, unknown to anyone, while the Gods raged among themselves like lightning and thunder in a torrential rainfall. They knew someone had helped the rebellious blasphemer and they could not find out who the helper was.

Sarai believed what the old man told the people. These men were big and strong, with powerful weapons, but they were not Gods. As the years passed, she had to learn to tolerate the voices in her head that told her their thoughts and secrets, even when they made her guts roil. She found that most of the time she could push their rough voices, their thoughts, their vulgar feelings, to the back of her mind if she concentrated hard enough on someone else or on some task she was required to do. One thing was clear to the little girl: the "Gods" did not love the people who served and worshipped them. The Gods used the people of Earth however it pleased them.

One night, unable to fall asleep as their *voices* stamped around in her head, Sarai crept out of the children's room and ran through the Temple on her bare feet, down the stone steps and through the lush gardens until she came to a deserted path. She paused, lifting each smarting foot in turn to brush away the pebbles and twigs that she had trodden upon in her haste to get away from the Temple. Alone in the silent night, she noticed the Gods' voices were fading. That was better, but they were still there. She would have to wait until they too lay down to sleep.

She covered her face with her hands and wept softly, then harder until she retched. How she wished she could run away from them! But she feared what they would do to her with their weapons when they found her. If everyone was afraid to join the old man when he defied the Gods, they would certainly not risk helping her escape the Gods' will and commands. She was only a girl, with no one in whom she could confide. Dear, sweet Melina had been terrified by what the child knew. Even she would never speak of it, although sometimes she kissed Sarai on the cheek, leaving her own tears on the troubled girl's smooth skin as proof that she felt deeply for her. Sarai did not dare ask, but she wondered if Melina too doubted the so-called Gods.

The Gods didn't seem to love each other either. They often fought and argued among themselves—unless they were drunk on the wine their worshippers made and brought to them, or pleasuring themselves with the beautiful chosen priestesses. The little girl hated their pleasuring most of all, for the Gods were much larger than the women of Earth and Sarai could *hear* a woman whimpering in the God's ears. Confused and frightened, young Sarai imagined the woman could barely breathe under the weight of the huge man.

Sarai grew tall and beautiful, with thick, shiny black hair, emerald eyes, soft olive skin and a comely figure. The Gods noticed her; her statuesque figure was enticing to them. She was only thirteen when, to her horror and revulsion, her Masters chose her, honored her as a priestess. She trembled with fear and loathing the first time one of them used her, but was surprised to find that he did not hurt her. She guessed this was because, just like the old man she remembered so well, she was taller and bigger than most of the people of the Earth. Also, because she could *hear* their repulsive thoughts and desires, she *knew* what to do to increase

7

and hasten their vulgar pleasure; usually that meant they would be through with her sooner. Unfortunately, it also made her their favorite priestess and she was often called to serve them.

At least she was rewarded afterward by being allowed to wander the city and the seashore for several hours on her own each day. Further from her Masters, their disgusting thoughts and voices faded from inside her head. Nestling her bottom into the warm sand and stretching out her strong, long legs, Sarai basked in the sun and the sweet relief of her daily escape. Sand sifted between her toes and her thighs, for her legs were bare. When she stood, the bottom of her short white tunic did not reach her knees. Her long, black hair fell loose to her hips when she did not tie it up or back. The Gods did not allow priestesses to cut off their hair unless it reached the ground and impeded their walking.

During the warm season, she loved to walk into the sea until it covered her like a watery cocoon. Then she let go as though she were falling and let the waters sway and caress her yielding body. It felt so familiar, as though she had long ago lived in the sea. For a brief time, she was at peace.

One day, sitting on the sand, staring at the breaking waves, she met the old apothecary. The woman was elderly, unusual that way as the old man had been. Her face was ugly, covered with warts; warts popped out from under her heavy, long robe, especially visible on her gnarled old hands. The two women chanced upon each other often at the ocean and became friends. Sarai learned that the old woman's name was Marusha and that she had extensively studied herbs. Some of this knowledge she had gained through talking to the human healers who ministered, under the Gods' direction, to those sick who came to the Temple for help.

Although she was careful to keep her *hearing* secret, Sarai realized that Marusha was the same wart-covered woman the Gods had derided that day long ago when Sarai discovered she could *hear* them. Under the guise of adoration of fat, sloppy Jor-Gum, bringing him offering after offering, Marusha had got to know the human healers and talked often to them of the study of herbs and healing. Unappreciative Jor-Gum never did reward her feigned worship by healing her warts, nor did Marusha ever learn to cure herself. However, she did gain much useful knowledge and one day she shared special wisdom with Sarai.

Marusha came to know the young priestess well enough to sense Sarai disdained her Masters and loathed serving them. Sarai would never dare speak of her disgust for the Gods—the old woman knew that well. But Sarai was perhaps Marusha's only true friend and the elderly one suspected the girl needed help with something about which she did not dare speak. So the old woman gifted the young woman from her heart.

"I will share a secret with you," she confided one day.

"A secret." Sarai smiled. "You honor me, my friend."

"Indeed," nodded the old herbalist, "as you honor me with your friendship." Her voice grew solemn as she continued, "You must never share this secret with anyone. The Gods would be angered."

The thought of the Gods' ire pleased the young priestess. It was her secret joy to *hear* their frustrations. However, she kept her face impassive, neither smiling nor breathing harder. She assured the woman, "Marusha, my friend, I will keep any secret you want to share with me."

Marusha's smile, only half-full of her rotting old teeth, parted the warts on her wrinkled cheeks. "You are my true friend, Sarai, and I want to give you this secret before I am too old to remember it myself. Come—come with me to my hut. I have much to show you."

They stood up, brushing the sand from their legs and clothing. Joining arms, they walked across the sand to a strand of huts on the dirt road bordering the beach. Marusha lived in one of these. Unlike many of the stinking hovels of the poor folk, Marusha's hut was fragrant with herbs. There was a plethora of smells which tickled the visitor's nostrils, some spicy, some sweet, some bitter, some pungent. There were so many jars and bags of herbs that the hut contained little more than these, a small hearth and a sleeping pallet on the dirt floor.

That afternoon, Sarai learned the secret that would keep the Gods from getting her with child. The herb was bitter and made her gag when she tasted it, even though her friend tried mixing it with sweeter plants. Kind Marusha knew where it grew and harvested it almost daily. From that day, she made sure Sarai had plenty of it so she could eat just a bit of dried herb after being called to serve the Gods. Soon after, she invited the priestess to accompany her to the hills where it grew. Sarai dared not speak of her immense gratitude, for her friend could not be endangered by knowing for sure how much she disdained her Masters. But she let her eyes tell Marusha as she grasped her wart-covered hands.

Three mornings after the old woman gifted her with the special herb, Sarai lost the child she was carrying. She even welcomed the cramping and heaved a sigh of relief at the sight of the bloody clumps. She had lost a child once before, when she was in her fourteenth spring. She had not even realized she was with child. She was terrified when the blood flowed with the cramping pain. With the sixth sense of one who deeply loves a child, Melina had found Sarai in the gardens where she desperately tried to hide. She had explained gently to the girl what was happening, advised her several times not to tell anyone else and helped her to clean herself up afterwards.

Dear Melina had been everything to young Sarai: mother, older sister, wise teacher, trusted friend. Less than a month after the first time Sarai lost a child, the older woman fell on the stone Temple steps, cracked her skull and died instantly. She was by then a rare old priestess and never called upon by the Gods. She was given the honored, ceremonial burial well deserved by a faithful priestess. Then she was soon forgotten, except by Sarai, who missed her every day. She mourned her sadly, bitterly. She did not care that the Gods saw her tears when they took her for their pleasure. The brutes were accustomed to the tears of the priestesses who served them and never guessed Sarai cried tears of grief.

She found some comfort in the serenity of the seashore and tarried there most days she was free to wander on her own. Not long after, she encountered Marusha at the beach and their developing friendship opened her eyes and her heart to new friends.

Taran became Sarai's closest friend. The Gods had brought her to the Temple in their thunderous metal sky chariot that rode across the heavens on blue and orange fire. Taran did not remember what it was like to fly through the skies within the huge chariot, for she had fallen asleep before the Gods took her from the village of her family. After the chariot's fires had lowered the craft to the landing platform at the back of the Temple, the God Jor-Gum had carried the new chosen priestess outside and set her in the grass before the assembled priestesses, who attended her when she woke.

Like the foundling Sarai, Taran was the only other priestess without family in the City below the Temple hill. Although Taran was perhaps a year older than she, Sarai was glad to guide her in the priestess duties, much as Melina had done when she was chosen as a priestess to the Gods. Taran, with her fair skin, bright blonde hair and confident blue eyes, attracted the Masters the way Sarai did: she was pretty and taller than most of the people of the Earth, although Sarai was still a head taller and more muscular. In contrast to Sarai, Taran was lithe and slender.

The girls adored each other the way best friends or sisters do and brought giggles and laughter to each other and those around them. When there were no Gods around they liked to do silly things, like having water fights, splashing each other in the garden fountains in a hilarious contest until they were breathless with effort and laughter. Although this was not considered dignified priestess behavior, their harmless antics did bring smiles to the lips of passers-by and no one stopped the fun. Since Sarai *knew* when one of the Gods approached, no God ever witnessed their play and the question of their disapproval never arose.

One spring day when she could already feel the heat of summer, Sarai looked for her friend Marusha at the beach and then walked to her herb-filled hut, hoping to find her at home. Yes, she was at home—she was still on her sleeping pallet, dead. The young woman's heart broke at the loss of her dear elderly friend, but she cried tears of gratitude that Marusha had passed away in peace after she lay down to sleep the previous night.

The weeping priestess found a large hemp bag that Marusha had often used to carry herbs or wood for her fire. Feeling great tenderness and respect, she gently moved her friend's frail body into the bag. Marusha had become thin and small in her unusual, advanced age; tall, strong Sarai did not have much trouble carrying the bundle to the field where their secret plant grew, although she wisely paused to rest at intervals along the way. Digging a grave with tree branches and stones took hours, however, so Sarai did not return to the Temple until nearly nightfall. This time Sarai did not have to grieve alone, for her friend Taran was there to comfort her in her loss. It was easier to share her sadness with another.

Some weeks later, without her beloved old friend Marusha, Sarai rested and pondered alone on the sands of the seashore. Usually she felt relieved to thrust her Masters from her mind as soon as she got far enough from them that their ugly *voices* faded away. But now in her eighteenth spring, her familiarity with the

Gods' secrets greatly troubled her. Digging her bare feet into the warm beach sand, she closed her eyes and knit her brows together. For all her power of *hearing* their thoughts, she could not understand why they had killed two priestesses who carried their children.

Twice in the last few weeks, the Gods had told the other priestesses that a priestess had suddenly taken ill and died. First Vesta and then Nila, both of them strong and healthy young women, although Nila had only begun her womanly bleeding last fall season just before the Gods chose her to serve them. Each time the Gods had killed a priestess, Sarai *knew* the woman was with child, because she *heard* that the Gods knew.

Regardless of age, it was unusual for a priestess to carry her child until birth; the baby died within her womb. Priestesses rarely gave birth and these babes were generally sickly and, like Melina's son who lived only seven days, did not survive infancy. One boy, called Blorn, had lived ten years and grown big and fat, but he was slow-thinking and needed constant care. He could barely dress himself. If his mother did not sit with him when he ate, he dropped most of his food down his robes and on the floor beneath him. Recently, the Gods reported that he had wandered off and could not be found. Sarai shuddered at their lie, for she knew that they had killed him, too.

Sarai surmised that a woman of the Earth was not large enough to nourish a child of these huge men. Nonetheless, for reasons she could not *hear*, the Gods now chose to kill any priestess who carried their child. She must find out why and more importantly she must find a way to warn the other priestesses without revealing her dangerous *hearing* secret. She knew where to find Marusha's special herbal protection. Though she felt guilty sharing it with other women after Marusha had made her promise not to reveal their shared knowledge, she felt she must somehow find a way to get the other priestesses to eat it. But how? Whatever could she do all on her own?

She thought about the brave old man. He was the only one who had openly dared to defy the Gods and he had escaped. There had to be a way to thwart them. She would not openly defy the Gods. No, her way would be quiet, secret as always; she must stop them and save the lives of the priestesses. She would find the way.

Two

When Sarai returned, Taran was waiting for her at the bottom of the steps leading up to the Temple. The blonde girl's cheeks flushed pink and her slate-blue eyes sparkled. Smiling sweetly, she tugged at Sarai's arm and breathed, "Sarai, I'm so glad you are back! Come with me, please hurry. I'm so excited! I have something wonderful to tell you."

Taran pulled Sarai into one of the adjacent gardens, not pausing until they stood behind a tall hedge of red roses. Sarai was mute, allowing her friend to lead her where she would. Something gnawed in the pit of her stomach. She knew what Taran would tell her. Nonetheless, she pretended to share her friend's excitement as they hid behind the hedge. She cupped a hand on each of her slender friend's shoulders. "So, tell me!" she begged. "What is it? What has happened?"

Taran jumped lightly on her toes in her excitement, but her dancing blue eyes still looked straight into Sarai's green ones. "I carry a child of the Gods!" she exclaimed in a loud whisper, clutching her hands together as if attempting to contain herself.

Sarai's throat went dry, but she asked hoarsely, "You are with child? Are you sure?"

"Oh, yes!" asserted her older friend. "I missed my monthly bleeding weeks ago and I was—sick—this morning. Oh, Sarai! It has been so long since a priestess has given birth to a child of the Gods. I *know* this child will be born. I feel it strongly."

Sarai choked back her anguish, swallowing her own spew. *No! This cannot be happening! I will not lose dear, sweet Taran.* Her thoughts raced as she desperately searched for a way to convince Taran to keep her pregnancy a secret. Forcing a wide smile, she hugged Taran to her and whispered conspiratorially into her ear, "How wonderful! Have you told anyone else?"

"Of course not," Taran replied, as she stroked Sarai's smooth, shiny hair with one hand. "I wanted you to be the first to know."

Sarai heaved a sigh of relief, which Taran did not seem to notice. *Then there is still time to save my best friend!* "Thank you, thank you for sharing the honor with me, Taran. But let's keep it a secret for a while longer. Let it be a surprise and it will be a greater joy! You will be much favored by all the Gods. Does anyone else know you were sick this morning?"

"Oh, no," replied Taran. "I was sitting right here really, behind the roses. I just wanted to feel the warm sunshine and then all of a sudden..." She released Sarai and acted as though she had to vomit.

"Good," said Sarai, keeping her voice even in tone. "Don't tell anyone until they notice. Maybe you will not be sick very much." She lowered her voice almost to a whisper. "Before she died,

Marusha told me about an herb. It makes you stronger, better able to carry your child. But she made me promise not to tell anyone about it, so I keep it hidden in my alcove. I really want you to have the herb's benefits and I don't think she would be angry if I shared it with you. Come sleep with me tonight so I can give you some."

Taran smiled, her eyes brilliant in her happiness. "Oh, thank you, Sarai! I knew you should be the first to know. Oh, but Sarai," she hesitated, wrinkling her nose, "I might be sick again. I would not want to be sick on your sleeping pallet…"

Sarai waved her arm in dismissal. "Don't worry about that, Taran. I have been sick that way before, but I lost my child."

"You did? Sarai, you never told me you carried a child of the Gods."

"Oh, it was so long ago. I was—I was not long serving the Gods and I know it was before they chose you to be a priestess. I didn't even know I was with child. I think I was too young. Too young and too weak to carry a child. Maybe I will never be able to carry a child," she lied, warming to her task of convincing Taran to share the special herb. "But you are older and stronger. You have not lost a child as I did. Let me help you! Let me share my wonderful herb with you."

Taran embraced Sarai and kissed her cheek. "Yes," she murmured. "Thank you, Sarai."

Sarai had more of the herb hidden in three places near the back of the Temple. She had stuffed three more of Marusha's endless supply of hemp cloths and bags (these bags were small, no bigger than her two hands side by side) with the precious weed and found spaces close to the ground between the great stones of the Temple walls in which to secrete her treasure. It was easy to find large rocks to cover the spaces, hiding them from sight. But there was no need to tell Taran about her hidden supply. She did not want her friend to suspect her true motives.

Though frantic with worry that the Gods would discover Taran carried a child, her heart also ached for the other dutiful priestesses. She wondered if she could convince them, too, that eating a little of the bitter herb would make them stronger child bearers. The lie was her best idea at present and she could still find plenty of the plant before the winter season was upon them. She would need to harvest a great amount of it before the cold rains started. Perhaps she would bring Taran with her to help—if Taran was lucky enough to lose her child before the Gods noticed her condition.

Sarai felt her belly flutter; she was queasy. She wished fervently that there truly was a God, even one God, to whom she could pray for help. Even if her plan succeeded, even if every one of the priestesses believed her gentle lie and was eager to use the protective herb, one of them might notice that no one remained with child. Even Taran might wonder if this herb was supposed to strengthen her when instead she lost her child soon after she ate some. Sarai could not know what might happen, but she knew she had to risk it.

After they had eaten the evening meal, Sarai and Taran clasped hands and skipped off to Sarai's alcove. As honored priestesses, they were not required to participate in nightly chores and clean-up, although they were free to do so and priestesses usually joined the servants in their duties. But a chosen priestess could retire to her own alcove as soon as she wanted. Unlike mere servants in the Temple who shared communal sleeping areas, a priestess was given a private alcove as soon as she was chosen by the Gods to serve them. Sarai was glad she could easily hide her secret herb in her own alcove without worrying that someone else would find it.

Holding tightly to her friend's hand, the tall, dark-haired priestess pulled aside the rich, red tapestry that separated her alcove from the rest of the Temple and led Taran inside. Only when the tapestry had fallen back into place did she release Taran's hand.

Taran looked around. Sarai's alcove was almost the same as hers, with walls, floors and a high ceiling hewn by the Gods from the same smoothed rock with which they had long ago built the rest of their Temple. The meager space was filled by a simple sleeping pallet, clean blankets and large baskets for storing the priestess's other few tunics, hairbrush and the like. There were thick woven straw mats under the sleeping pallet and covering most of the hard rock floor, providing comfort as well as warmth in the cool rock alcove. A wide-mouthed jug of fresh water always stood near the entrance. However, in this particular alcove, opposite the red tapestried entrance was a small opening in the rock, a window not much bigger than one of the Gods' large heads, which looked down upon the main market area in the city below the hill where the Temple stood.

Sarai immediately stepped over her sleeping pallet and peered out. She loved to stand there, gazing out at the people moving through the city, recognizing those she had seen more than once. She wished she lived among them, maybe with her own parents, brothers and sisters. During the winter season, she kept the window tightly covered with animal furs bound over it. The Gods had built the Temple roof to slope down beyond the alcove's wall, providing additional protection from the rains but still allowing a view down the hill. Now that the weather was mild, she only covered the window at night with a small, light blue tapestry.

"Have you seen the new mother again, the one with two babies?" asked Taran.

Sarai sighed, untied the rope that held up the blue tapestry and let it fall over the opening. "No," she answered, turning to Taran. "Now I'm not even sure I saw the babies. It's so far away. Hard to see as much as I'd like to see. Sometimes I wish…"

"Oh, Sarai," Taran soothed, "you will have a child, too. I know you will. The Gods honor you so often."

Sarai smiled at Taran and then stepped toward the basket in the corner. There was little point in telling Taran she dreamt of bearing the child of her own husband, of living with the people in the city below this great stone Temple of the Gods. She would never carry their child, nor would Taran if either of them was to remain alive. She shoved the straw basket aside, got to her knees and with both hands moved aside a heavy rock. The herb was behind it, covered with one of Marusha's old hemp cloths.

Taran gagged on the bitter herb and nearly spat it out. She hastily reached for the water jug and gulped as water trickled down her chin into the folds of her white tunic. Sarai, now accustomed to the strong taste after eating the herb so often, had forgotten how bad it had tasted when she first sampled it in Marusha's hut. She had long ago stopped eating it in combination with other food. Besides, her little alcove did not have much room for storage. To encourage Taran she ate some herself, as if sharing the bitter taste with her friend might make the acrid stuff easier to swallow.

Determined Taran managed to chew and swallow the required amount, following it with liberal swigs from the water jug. Still grimacing after she had finished, she rubbed the small of her back with one hand. Sarai replaced the herb bag in the corner and moved the heavy stone back in front of it. Reaching into one of the large baskets, she pulled out two tan-colored sleeping shifts and gave one to Taran.

"Your back hurts," she said, noticing the strain in Taran's face.

"Yes," Taran nodded, closing her eyes. "I've been tired. I shouldn't be surprised, but I'm just not used to how I feel. I'm glad it's almost dark. I'll be asleep before the light's gone." She opened her eyes to pull on her sleeping shift.

"Lie down. I'll rub your back," Sarai offered.

"Oh, thank you, Sarai. I'm just so tired…" Her voice trailed off as she lay down on her side. In the dim light, Sarai could just make out her long yellow hair spilling down her back and onto the mat.

Sarai sat down next to her. Taran pulled her shift above her hips and indicated the sore area with one hand before she let it fall in front of her. Sarai touched her fingertips near the curve of the slender girl's waist and watched them glide over the pale flesh toward Taran's hip and buttock. Then she gently kneaded and rubbed the area. She paused, lifting her hands just above the quiet figure. Then she stroked the long, yellow hair. It felt almost watery in its smoothness, so unlike her own thick black hair. She stroked Taran's back again and shyly traced the curve of her hip with one hand. Closing her eyes, she drew in her breath, then slowly released it. She felt her heart pulsing in her throat. Bolder, she opened her eyes and reached under the light garment to stroke the length of Taran's back with both hands, down to her rounded buttocks and back up to her narrow shoulders.

Sarai massaged the small of the other girl's back again. Her voice husky, she asked, "Does this help? Does it feel good?"

Taran did not answer. Sarai leaned over until her ear caught the whisper of the girl's breath; she had probably fallen asleep with the first touch of Sarai's fingers. Smiling, Sarai grasped the rumpled blanket at Taran's feet and pulled it over them both as she lay down on her back next to the friend she loved more than anyone else. In the new darkness, Taran breathed a little louder, steadier. Sarai slowed her own breathing to match Taran's. She fell asleep.

THREE

She opened her eyes to morning sunlight filtering through the blue window tapestry and the cracks between the boulders that made up the rock walls. She felt for Taran with one hand, but she was not there beside her. Hearing a low moan, she sat up and her eyes found Taran near the red tapestry.

The girl's blue eyes were tearing as she sat cross-legged on the straw mat, clutching the water jug to her chest. "Thought I might wake you," she mumbled. She tugged the top of her sleeping shift up to her face and wiped her mouth; her voice was muffled by the garment. "Ugh. I was afraid this would happen."

"Oh Taran. You were sick again."

Taran pulled the soiled shift below her chin. "Yes. I got up to go out and pass my water and then—well, you know. But look at this: I managed to get most of it into your water jug. Or down the sides, anyway."

"Don't worry. We can clean this up easily and get another water jug." Sarai crawled to Taran. She knelt, pulled her own sleeping shift over her head and dabbed at her friend's clammy forehead with it.

24

"I'm not worrying. I'm too busy feeling sick." Taran gave a short laugh. "I don't know how long I can hide this from everybody."

"Oh, but you must," Sarai urged, her voice quavering. She hoped Taran didn't notice. "It will be so much better if the others don't know yet. I will give you more of the herb to eat now. That will help."

"Ugh. I can't eat anything, especially that bitter herb."

"Of course. I'm going to give you some to keep in your alcove, for later. If one of the Gods calls you to serve him, eat some of it afterwards."

"Yes, I will. But Sarai, do you have enough left for yourself?"

"I can get more." Sarai finished wiping the sides of the water jug and stuffed her soiled shift into its mouth so it stuck out of the top. "Looks like the jug is throwing up." She laughed.

"Glad you think it's funny. I didn't want you to have to clean up after me." Taran got to her feet.

"Oh, it wasn't anything. You can sleep here again tonight if you want."

"You're so kind. But I'll stay in my alcove tonight." Taran pulled on her tunic. "I really have to pass my water. I'd better go and wash quickly. I will probably be called to serve." She took a step back to Sarai and gently hugged the naked woman.

"Wait. Take the herb." Sarai stooped and pulled away the rock in the corner to reach the herb bound in the cloth. "I can get more today. Just shove it under a mat in your alcove until you have time to hide it better."

Taran accepted the bundle and with a smile exited the alcove.

Sarai dressed quickly, collected the soiled shifts and water jug and went out to make her own preparations for the day. As she expected, the Gods called for both Taran and her later that morning. During the afternoon, she discreetly secured more of her secret herb from her hiding places outside. Sighing, she hoped the herb would do its work on Taran during the night, for both Sarai and Taran were favorite playthings of the Gods and were likely to be called to serve the Masters again before long.

The following morning, Taran felt sick again and could not eat her morning meal. She had not yet risen from the table when the God Scrae-Lon entered the meal hall to call for her. Sarai hugged her and whispered into her ear a reminder to eat some of the strengthening herb after her service to the God. But Taran barely heard her friend as she colored prettily at her God's attention and hastily got to her feet. Curling a bony finger in his scant yellow-white beard, the God Scrae-Lon smiled thinly as he watched her approach. Extending a pale hand, he drew her close to his long brown robes and led her away.

For a short time, Sarai busied herself helping the servants in their duties, hoping this would be the rare day none of the Gods called for her. The Gods' *voices* began digging between her ears again, arguing among themselves, distracting her even when she was called by the God Run-Gon. The burly, brown-haired God flashed his blue eyes approvingly at her as she came to his side, but Sarai fixed her gaze on the bottom of his green robe as she accompanied him to his chamber. As she served him, the hateful *voices* of the other Gods grew loud between her ears. Her belly

26

knotted up when she recognized they were yelling at each other about Taran, but she could not *understand* the words they used. Did they know? Had they discovered she was with child? She was relieved that it was not long before Run-Gon was through with her. He soon fell asleep on his spacious, raised sleeping pallet.

Sarai crept out of his chamber and dashed back to her own alcove to eat her portion of Marusha's herb. She trembled and hugged herself tightly, as if she could make herself be still. When she gagged on the plant, she hastily gulped down some water. She had to find Taran.

Oblivious to her pounding heart and the hard stone floor beneath her bare feet, Sarai paced through the Temple, searching for Taran. The Gods' *voices* were weaker now, almost gone from her thoughts, as though the Gods had left the Temple. And she still could not find her poor friend! She wished she could *hear* Taran's *inner voice* the same way she could *hear* the Gods, but she had never *heard* anyone but the Masters. Pausing to lean against one of the massive columns at the Temple entrance, she squeezed her eyes shut, desperately trying to *hear* what the Gods *were saying* about Taran.

"Oh good, I have found you, Sarai."

Sarai opened her eyes to see a small priestess who was dark-haired like herself. Looking down into Elia's wide brown eyes, she suppressed a groan of annoyance: she was in no mood for Elia's constant prattle about 'our Gods who love us so much.'

Elia reached for Sarai's hands and squeezed them. "I have been looking for you. I thought you would want to know about Taran.

I know she is like your sister."

"What is it? Did something happen to Taran?"

"I'm not sure if something happened to her. But I think she is sick. I was carrying food to the God—oh, why can't I think of His name? The God—"

"Never mind who it was!" Sarai snapped, fighting the impulse to shake her. "What did you see?"

"She was going into our God Scrae-Lon's chamber and she stopped and held her belly and she—was sick."

"What happened then? Did Scrae-Lon see her? Did anyone else see her?"

"I—I don't know. My God was calling me to bring his food and I couldn't stay to help her. I've been worried about her! I thought you would be worried, too. Have you seen her? Did you know she was sick?"

Sarai never answered. Weeping, she sank to her knees. Although she had tried to push her fear to a corner of her mind, tried to blind herself to the pictures behind her eyes, she finally admitted to herself she *knew*. She knew the cruel Masters had argued about whether to put to death one of their favorite priestesses. A few of them—even fat Jor-Gum—opposed it, but most of them, led by a disgusted Scrae-Lon, insisted on following what they called *the Rule*. A-Don, the tallest and their leader, had joined the group of quarreling Gods and decided the matter. *The Rule,* he insisted, *must be followed. It is the safest way. The Home World must not know of the abominations. I will attend to this.* Then he and Scrae-Lon took Taran away from the Temple to some place Sarai did not know, some place where she could no longer *hear* them. But she was sure they had killed Taran.

Elia knelt beside Sarai and put her arm around the other priestess's shoulders. "Sarai, are you also sick?" she asked in innocent concern.

"No," Sarai choked through her sobs, keeping her face turned to the ground.

"Are you sure? Many of the priestesses have been getting sick this year. We don't know what is ailing us."

Sarai felt as though she had been beaten to the ground by hot winds. Her skin seemed to burn as she forced herself to say, "I am not sick. I am leaving now—the Gods have awarded me my freedom for the afternoon." Springing up like a jackrabbit she raced outside, down the Temple steps and fled to the ocean. She dove into the crashing waves, wishing she had the courage to drown herself. She had lost all hope; she could not defeat her hated Masters by herself and who would believe her if she tried to tell the others what these "Gods" really thought? Her rage scorched through her like a wildfire, despite the cooling sea waters. With a sudden burst of determination she let herself sink under the water, her mouth open to take in the sea so she might find the sweet release of death. But her life instinct was too strong. Choking, coughing, gagging out the water she had swallowed, she pushed off the ocean floor as though her legs had a will of their own. Bursting out of the water, she drew in a huge breath of life-giving air.

Defeated, she dragged herself to shore and fell to the ground. Not even her bitter tears would come to release her grief. Burning like wood in the fire, she was consumed with hatred for the evil men who had killed her beloved friend. She vowed to destroy those who took everything from her and from the other unsuspecting people of the Earth. She chose to live for vengeance. Her *Rule* would be to kill every last one of them!

FOUR

The day after Taran's disappearance, the God A-Don addressed the priestesses when they were gathered in the dining hall for their morning meal. The illness had suddenly come upon Taran early the past day, he told them solemnly. Thankfully, she had not suffered long for she died before the sun was high in the sky. And since Taran was an honored and favored priestess to the Gods, there was to be a ceremonial burial for her this very afternoon.

Her green eyes hard and reddened from constant crying, Sarai watched the proceedings in the Temple garden from the back of a group of sorrowful young women. Richly attired in their fine robes, the Gods faced them from the opposite side of the gravesite. Taran's silent corpse, dressed only in a clean, white tunic and surrounded by her long yellow hair, was lowered into the sacred ground reserved for the burial of honored priestesses. Prayers were said; solemn songs were sung.

Sarai never opened her mouth to join in with the rest. Alone with her rage, she focused on each evil God in turn, wishing great pain and death on each until it seemed to her that several of them squirmed as though they indeed felt pain. Jor-Gum grimaced as he rubbed his fat belly. Scrae-Lon slapped at his neck as though mosquitoes were biting it. A-Don, the leader, speaking solemnly about laying Taran to rest in the earth, grew red and sweaty in the face although he kept his voice even. It was a hot, humid day and each of the Masters was clad in his customary thick, colorful robe. It could easily have been the heat that made them uncomfortable. Perhaps bugs were biting Scrae-Lon, sucking his dirty blood. Unlike the servile priestesses who were commanded and trained to appear calm during the most distressing of circumstances—such as witnessing the burning of a rebellious blasphemer—these "Gods" knew no such discipline. They were soft and lazy; even the heat irritated them.

During the long months that followed, Sarai dragged herself through her priestess duties and fled to the sea whenever she was free to escape there. She was mute most of the time, speaking only when a God addressed her and then only briefly to follow his commands. She wept openly and every day and no one tried to cheer her up except for concerned Elia, who buzzed around her like a persistent fly until Sarai wished she could slap her away. She preferred to keep to herself, obsessing over how to kill the Masters.

Aware of her love and friendship for Taran, some of the Gods left her alone to mourn and did not call on her to worship them. *A happier woman will do just as well,* she *heard* them say, with careless shrugs of their shoulders. But most of them insisted on calling on their favorite priestess. The God Sh'Baal even attempted to be gentle with her when he took her, although Sarai's tears never stopped. When he finished with her, sloppy and sweaty in his release, he rolled off her. Numb, Sarai turned to the wall and continued to cry quietly. Like dry, choking sand, hatred stuck in her throat for each of the heartless men who had murdered her friend. She would kill them all, when the time was right.

One day, after she had forced herself to eat part of the midday meal, she and the other priestesses heard the loud humming and thundering that signaled the approach of a chariot of the Gods. The arrival of their adored Gods from the Heavens above was always an exciting event. When they neared the Temple plateau, the people from the city below often came up to join the priestesses and Temple servants in greeting their beloved Masters.

Sarai joined the crowd of curious priestesses and servants who thronged outside to watch the roaring, groaning metallic chariot descend to the Earth on blue and orange flames until it settled on the landing platform behind the Temple. The chariot was smaller than usual and the God who emerged from it was not as tall as the other Gods living at the Temple. Nodding to them, he called out a greeting and said he was called Z'Shar.

Besides being a little shorter than the other huge men, his skin was darker. Most of the Gods had pale, even pinkish skin, but Z'Shar was darker, browner—like Sarai. His hair and beard were black and his eyes were very dark brown. In contrast to the ostentatious garb of her Masters, this God wrapped himself in a plain black cloak and wore a loose shirt, trousers and boots, also plain and black. He was quiet, greeting the other Gods who came to welcome their visitor with a polite smile and a brief word. His *voice* was not rough, did not hammer in her head as did the *voices* of the other Gods. She thought, *he's different—he's not like the other Gods. He—*

Suddenly she felt his eyes on her, deep and dark. And then it was quiet. She *heard* nothing from him. Apparently she had imagined his *voice* because he intrigued her. She shrugged, undecided if she was disappointed or relieved. If she could not hear this God, then that was one less heinous *voice* invading her thoughts—sickening her. Perhaps he really was not vile like the others; there seemed a gentleness about him. If her long-awaited opportunity came, she would not kill this one. After all, he was a stranger and not one of the Masters who had murdered Taran, Blorn the slow-minded child and the other priestesses whom they had gotten with child.

In the days that followed, she still *heard* nothing from this strange God and she grew nervous about him, as though tiny bugs were crawling on her back and she could not see them no matter how she twisted and turned. Having grown accustomed to *hearing* the Gods, she now felt vulnerable to this quiet one. There was no reason for her fears, she chided herself. The God Z'Shar kept mainly to himself as he walked through the Temple, speaking only briefly and officially with the other Gods.

He left the Temple grounds and wandered around the city every day. Sarai watched him surreptitiously through her tapestried window as he descended the Temple steps and walked casually into the marketplace. She saw that he smiled and greeted people he encountered. The humble people were honored by his presence among them and beamed with love and joy when he graced them with his smile, his attentions. Sarai was mystified: none of the Gods had ever behaved in so gracious a manner with the Earth people. He seemed to be a friend to them.

Even stranger, he never called a priestess to worship him. If he passed them within the Temple or in the gardens, he spoke kindly to the devoted women, just as he did with the adoring multitudes in the marketplace. Once she caught him staring at her, as if he were *listening* to her from behind his dark eyes. When she boldly stared back, he nodded and turned away. Sarai thought her imagination was running wild again, for like the rest of the Gods, this one could not *hear* her thoughts. But it was unnerving because she could not *hear* this visiting God's *voice,* so she could not anticipate what he would do. Her lip curled disdainfully and she didn't care if he noticed. Likely he was examining her, deciding whether he would command her to worship him. It was probably only a matter of time before he too called for a priestess.

But like an errant breeze her attitude toward him changed constantly. He was definitely a stranger, apparently only here to visit one of the Temple homes of the Gods on the Earth. Sarai knew there were other Temples where other Gods lived. She wondered where this God had come from and if there were other quiet Gods who looked and acted like him. Knowing that many people of the Earth looked very different from each other, it made sense to her that these Gods from what she'd *heard* them call *"Home World"* might also look very different from each other—

might even be kinder, nobler men. Certainly there must also be women among them, women to bear their children, to love and care for the children. Perhaps they were not all vile—

No! She hated them all. She would never forgive the horrible things they had done. She knew they were only here on Earth to use the people who worshipped them. She would never allow herself to forget the truth the old man had spoken.

Some days later, fat Jor-Gum called her to serve him. Afterwards, granted freedom to be on her own, Sarai rushed to get away from her rough Masters and their despised *voices* that filled her head. She fled blindly down the Temple steps, trusting her feet to re- member the familiar course they had taken so many times. She never saw the new God before she collided with him. Though he stood firm, Sarai fell to her hands and knees. Choking with fright, she knelt at his bare feet. She kissed his toes and begged, "Please forgive me, O Worshipped One! I will never forget You in my thoughts again! Allow me to serve You, to make amends for my transgression."

The God Z'Shar bent down and gently pulled her up, taking her chin in his hand to force her to look into his dark eyes. Sarai held her breath, flushed with shame. Her green eyes filled with tears, but she dared not look away. As he held her gaze captive, the God smiled and said kindly, "You have done me no harm. Do not be afraid. I am glad to have this chance to talk with you."

Sarai trembled at his unexpected kindness. This God was not like the others. She could not *hear* him. What would he do? What did he want from her?

This is what I want, she *heard* suddenly. Her knees buckled and, terrified, she wet herself. But he held her firmly so she did not fall on the steps. Keeping his eyes on hers, he continued, *I want you to know that I can hear you and you can hear me, too.*

Yes, my Lord!

Sarai, be at peace. Do not fear. No one else can hear us and I will tell no one. It is rare that I encounter another who hears. This is what I search for. I did not want to frighten you, so I kept my voice from you until now. I only want to share with you, to know you. Does that please you?

Yes, my God. Whatever You desire pleases me.

Sarai, I know your thoughts. You know I am no God, only a taller man.

Sarai's eyes widened at his unexpected confession. He had been *listening* to her since he arrived! Her legs shook so that her knees knocked together and she would have fallen had he not been holding her up. The man smiled into her eyes and then, inexplicably, she *felt* his tender caring for her, surrounding her, cradling her inside. Comforted, she ceased to shake. She was not afraid.

He laughed. His fingers left her chin to lightly stroke her hair. He *spoke* to her again. *You will have to continue calling me 'God' and 'Lord' out loud, for the others cannot know we share this. You know it is not safe for the others to know.*

Does no one else hear as we do, my Lord?

No one here, Sarai. There are others, far from here. I will tell you more when there is more time. But now, remember I am not your master. My name is Z'Shar. Do me the favor of calling me by my name.

Yes, Z'Shar, certainly I will.

"Good," he said aloud. "That makes me happy." He paused, smiling at her again. Taking her hand lightly in his, he invited her to sit on the steps with him. Sarai squirmed as she sat on the stone step, ashamed she had wet her tunic and her legs.

Don't worry, he *assured her kindly. There is no shame between us when we hear each other. Sarai, I must leave this place soon. There are things I want to tell you, but I don't know if there is time. I may find you by the ocean or pretend to call you to worship me. Although the others may demand all your attention, so I don't think I will get that chance.*

Sarai blushed at the thought of this gentle man touching her, taking his pleasure with her. She felt her womanly parts make ready for him. Shaken by her strange desirous feelings, her face reddened further and she lowered her eyes.

Z'Shar laughed and *said, I must teach you to block your thoughts. You should be free to keep your secrets from me.*

Sarai wished she could laugh too, but found herself crying. The man was so kind to her. She had never been able to share her thoughts with anyone else before. It felt good, very good. This man understood her. He was like her, in a way no one else had ever been like her. She was no longer alone.

Z'Shar took the end of his long black cloak in his hand and patted the tears from her eyes and flushed cheeks. *There are not many like us,* he *said. But there is a place… We cannot stay here longer. The others will notice. Go now—I will find you another day.* Aloud he said, "Go now, priestess. I look forward to your worship."

Sarai rose obediently, brought the bottom of his cloak to her lips and kissed it. She turned and ran down the Temple steps. His *laughter* followed her to the lip of the sea.

FIVE

Z'Shar did not find her the next day, for he was gone. He had climbed into his chariot during the night and fled, no one knew where. The furious *voices* of the other Gods were loud in Sarai's head, raging that Z'Shar had deceived them.

That abominable mutant is not allowed among us! A-Don informed the other Gods.

He's a mutant! exclaimed one. *Of course—we should have seen that. He spent more time among the people down in the city than here with us.*

Not only that, A-Don seethed, *but he's been banished to stay here on this miserable world, forbidden to return to the Home World. They found out he is one of those mutants who can hear your thoughts. Somebody on the other side of the big ocean heard him tell the Earth people we are not their Gods.*

Jor-Gum spat. *I hate those weird mutants! How could he have fooled us?*

How were we to know he'd been banished? I thought he was one of those weak little officials, visiting and inspecting for the Home World. He was wearing the standard traveling suit, Sh'Baal said, explaining his thoughts.

Scrae-Lon spoke up. *Remember the old man who disappeared? Yes, that was many years ago. This damned mutant probably took him away! I've heard they can do that—disappear like that. How long has he been here? Are there more of them, sneaking around right in front of us? Ugh. They're unnatural, filthy. They should be exterminated.*

A-Don muttered agreement. *We'll get him if he comes here again. Or we'll find him and kill him.*

We'll be helping everyone from Home World! asserted another God, Bik-Rud. *I don't care if he is supposed to be our kind. He's worse than these stupid Earth people. At least they can't fight us.*

Home World would reward us, Run-Gon said. *Most people believe those Listeners should be eradicated.*

Look, he's no fool, said their leader, resignation in his voice. *We should have caught on to him before. He never called for a priestess.*

Dismayed, Sarai sat up on her sleeping pallet, alone in her private alcove. She would never see Z'Shar again! He was the only one who had ever *heard* her, the only one who had ever *spoken* with her. Suddenly, she desired him again and she blushed hotly. With a heavy sigh, she reminded herself he really was one of them, the ones she detested—those who had killed Taran. Perhaps he did seek to help the people, but he was not of the Earth. So it was better this way. Yes, better, she reminded herself.

She was not comforted. She squirmed, battling her feelings. If he was not of Earth as she was, then why did he seem more like her than anyone she had ever known? In one short talk, he had come to know her better than her dearest loves, Marusha, Taran and Melina. She was like him; she was different in the same way

41

he was different. She supposed the people of Earth would call her a mutant too if they knew what she could *hear*. But she could only hear the Gods, the men from Home World. Why was that? Who was she, really? Her parents were unknown, her background a mystery.

Sarai felt her stomach juices rise into her throat. She gulped, forcing them down. *What if I am like Blorn, fathered by one of the Gods?* She got to her hands and knees and rocked back and forth, back and forth, unable to stop her own thoughts. She could not *hear* her own kind. Who else could she be? Was her mother also of the Gods? Where was her mother? Had she come from Home World?

No, it was more likely her mother was of the Earth. Then she, Sarai, was like Blorn, but somehow not dull and slow as he had been. Blorn had been a big, heavy child and Sarai was taller and probably stronger than most of the men she had seen in the city below. She pushed herself to her knees and clutched her belly, retching, wishing she could vomit up her misery. The idea was unbearable! She would go mad if she kept thinking about it.

Squeezing her eyes shut, she concentrated on the violent storm outside. The pounding rains had come suddenly in the night, relentless from the very start. Awakening to shouts in the morning, she had raised the tapestry and peered below to the flooded marketplace. Only a few people were about, bending forward against the angry downpour, working feverishly to take down their tents and save what they could of their goods.

Now, from her pallet, she glanced up to the uncovered opening in the wall. Lightning flashed across the clouded sky and thunder rolled in on the darkness that followed. Even the heavy stone walls of the Temple seemed to groan under the rain's onslaught. To avoid the terrible questions in her mind, Sarai made herself listen to the crying of the skies.

She had cried when she buried Marusha. It had been nothing to her to hoist the large hempen bag over her back, to carry Marusha all the way to the field where the precious herb grew. She didn't need any help. The male servants of the Temple sought *her* help when they had heavy loads to haul. She always helped them bring in the logs for the fires built in the great hearths when the winters were cold. While the rest of the women just watched or did other tasks, Sarai heaved and pulled with the men. *I am so big.* That was why the Gods chose her. They liked her because she was one of them.

No. *No!* Desperate to shut out her thoughts, she let her *hearing* wander back to the Gods. She would *listen* to them again. Better to *hear* their thoughts than to be tortured by her own.

I hate this rain, complained Jor-Gum. *Why is there so much rain in the middle of the hot season?*

Be glad it just started here, said Lew-Ron, one of the tallest Gods. *I heard from Mill-Us in the station—no, two stations east of us—that there's flooding in the valleys. Animals are drowning and people too. Mill-Us said there isn't enough food, even for us Gods.* He snickered.

I talked to him too, said the God Bin-Duss. *Mill-Us told me about a man—a man big for one of them, like Sarai. This man built a huge wooden boat to float on the waters. He calls it an ark. He claimed God told him how to build it.*

What God? asked Lew-Ron. *Which one of us would tell him to build—oh, was it that mutant?*

No, not that, said Bin-Duss, starting to laugh. *Listen to this: the earthling says there is only this one, all-powerful God that nobody can even see.* He guffawed and the others laughed with him.

He must be mad, said Jor-Gum with a snort.

There's more, Bin-Duss continued. *The great invisible God told him to gather up his entire family—sons, wives, everybody—and all kinds of animals and get them all into this ark because everyone here on Earth, even us 'other Gods', we're all going to die. We're all going to drown in a huge flood!* He broke off, laughing again.

But they're going to ride around in the big wooden boat and be the only ones alive when the rain stops, sneered Scrae-Lon.

Sounds like they'll have plenty of meat, joked Sh'Baal. *But I'll bet this fool and his ark is going to be somebody's problem over there at our eastern station.*

The thunder was gone now and the rain had lessened to a patter, but Sarai's head ached from the roar of the Masters' laughter. She pressed her palms on either side of her head, wishing she could squeeze the *voices* between them into silence.

Hmmm… Scrae-Lon mused out loud, *thinking of big earthlings, I'm going to call for Sarai.*

No! Not now. She could not bear it. Wearing only her short tunic, Sarai rushed from her alcove, raced down the Temple steps into the rain and ran towards the beach. She went to Marusha's hut. Even though her friend was gone, Sarai still liked to visit her old home. Except for the bugs and rats who kept her company she could be alone there, only her own voice inhabiting her mind. She arrived soaking wet, but inside it was quite dry, only a few leaks. Marusha had known how to build a durable roof, but it would not last another year with so much rain.

SIX

Sarai heard the rain pelting harder on the old roof. Two drops plopped on her nose. Uncrossing her wet legs, she crawled towards Marusha's sleeping pallet and sat on the damp ground amid the old, rotting rushes. She could not stay here through the night, but she was not ready to leave. She pondered how she could kill the Gods. It would be best to get hold of one of their fire-sticks. Over the years she had *listened* to them as they employed the weapons to suit their purposes. She already knew how to use the long metal flame-throwers.

The Gods kept their weapons hidden somewhere in the inner chambers of the Temple. Sometimes she could *see* one of them replacing his weapon in one of the metal boxes in which they were stored. But like all who served the Gods, Sarai had never dared venture beyond the meeting hall with the great hearth. The inner chambers were forbidden to all but the Gods. Now she must *listen* very carefully so she might learn to find her way by stealth and seize one of their fire-throwers.

A brilliant flash of lightning lit up the old hut, revealing sandy puddles of water at its edges. Several cockroaches scurried around her across the rushes. The thunder crash that followed seemed to shake the entire shack and then she could hear nothing but the pounding rain. She could stay there no longer.

Squinting through sheets of rain, Sarai leaned into the wind and slowly made her way back up the hill to the Temple. Though night had not yet fallen, she found most of the priestesses and servants gathered before the great hearth, sharing the evening meal early together. She saw they had brought their sleeping pallets before the fire. As they often did when winter nights were cold, they would sleep close together to stay warm and dry.

Relieved to see that Sarai had returned, Elia and two other priestesses rushed to greet her. Still dripping rain, her tunic clinging to her flesh, Sarai returned their hugs and accepted the bread they offered. Elia took her free arm and led her close to the hearth. They sat. Sarai crossed her legs and sighed as the fire warmed her. She chewed contentedly on the bread.

Someone cried out. As Sarai twisted to look behind, Elia and the others around her were already scrambling to their feet. Suddenly, a hard fist pounded into the side of her head. Her ears rang; her eyes clouded. Someone grabbed her arm and yanked her to her feet. She tottered to the side and the bread fell from her lips, but the rough hand held her up. Eyes clearing, she raised her head to stare at the God Scrae-Lon. Snarling, he slapped her face, hard. Tears filled her eyes. She drew a huge breath and wrenching herself from his grasp took two steps back.

The Master's face flushed red against his pale, yellow-white hair. "Stay where you are!" he commanded, his voice echoing in the great hall.

She stood, grinding her teeth, her eyes fixed on his thin face.

"Where were you?" he demanded. She did not answer. He lowered his voice and spat, "Priestess, you are here to serve the Gods. You were not here when I came for you. Where did you go?"

Save for her heaving breath, Sarai remained silent. She lowered her eyes and contemplated her adversary. Could she run from him if he decided to strike her again? Unlikely. However strong she was, the God was still bigger and could easily catch and over-power her. *But he is gaunt, thinner than the rest of them. When he takes his pleasure with me, I could get my big hands around his neck while he sleeps afterward and squeeze the breath from him.*

"Priestess, you will answer your God!" Scrae-Lon roared. He raised his fist to beat her again.

Reckless with rage, Sarai glared at him and raised her arms to fend off the blow. She bared her teeth. *If you hit me again,* she thought wildly, *I will choke the life from you right now!*

The God hesitated, fist in the air. He caught his breath and his other hand went protectively to his bearded throat. Quickly, he brought his hand back to his side, balling his fingers into another fist. His eyes narrowed as he hissed, "You will never leave the Temple again. I forbid you! You will serve me when I call for you. If I decide to let you live, you will be punished."

A huge clap of thunder rolled through the Temple. The God Run-Gon, fire-stick in hand, appeared in front of her. He grabbed

Scrae-Lon by the shoulder. "Scrae-Lon! Come. A-Don is speaking to us."

Rigid, Scrae-Lon opened his fist and pointed at Sarai. "She must be punished."

Run-Gon's eyes flicked to Sarai. "So. She has returned. Later—call for her later. Do what you will. There is no time now."

"Stay here!" Scrae-Lon barked the order. "I will return when I am ready." The two Gods turned and took long strides away, almost as though they had forgotten the transgressor.

Sarai slowly lowered her arms. But she could not move. Her buttocks were knotted like the fists that had just menaced her; her thighs shook. She glanced around the hall: it was empty, except for the tumbled sleeping pallets and the food left behind by the servants and priestesses as they fled from the angry God. She blinked. She had not known she was alone with Scrae-Lon. She forced a foot forward, then the other. She would not wait for him, nor would she ever again serve any Master who called for her.

She paused by the great hearth, breathing more slowly, deeper. She knew they would punish her, try to beat her into submission. They would probably kill her. Let them try. Let them do it. She knew she could take at least one of them with her. Scrae-Lon had shown her how. She would get her hands around the neck of one of them.

SEVEN

The rains did not stop. Brilliant lightning, huge jagged knives of light followed by booming thunder announced more pounding rain. Sarai stood, lost in thought, by the fire. Looking in all directions like frightened mice, the people of the Temple crept back into the hall. When they saw no Gods, they fell upon the lone priestess with hugs and caresses. They begged her to stop her madness, to obey the great Gods lest they strike her dead. "Come, have food to eat and sleep with us near the fire," they urged her, "and you will be warmed and made well again."

"No," she told them. "I am not mad. I am warm enough. It is not winter. I must be alone."

It would have to be enough for them that they saw her alive. She had no time to quiet their concern, to soothe Elia's fears for her life. She would not let them see Scrae-Lon punish her. She would not risk him harming others when he came to get her, or worse, to kill her. She consented to share the rest of the evening meal with them and sat with them, but said little. Feeling how much she loved them, her tears fell.

Scrae-Lon did not return for her. Moreover, they heard nothing from any of the Gods while Sarai sat with them. Perhaps that was only because the roaring rains drowned out any sounds except those of the people sharing food before the fire. When she had eaten her fill, Sarai stood and promised to join them again for the morning meal. She told herself she must eat quickly then, for she did not want to be among them if Scrae-Lon came.

She needed to be alone with her *hearing*. She did not lie down to sleep in her alcove but sat, legs crossed, on her sleeping pallet and *followed* the Gods into their thoughts, *seeing* where they went and what they were doing. The leader A-Don spoke often, instructing them in what he wanted each to do, though his *words* held no meaning for her. Nor could she understand what the other Gods *said,* nor why they were moving strange metal boxes throughout the stormy night towards the innermost chamber where their great chariot stood.

Above her alcove, the unending rain sounded like gravel being poured down by some great God in the Heavens. But no sound interfered with what Sarai *heard* and *saw* between her ears. She sat still, continuing to *listen* to the Gods as they approached the great chariot.

This was the first time she had *seen* the great chariot through their eyes. The Gods did not travel in that chariot; they used the smaller, rounded ones which easily landed on the platform behind the Temple. Like the round chariots, this giant cylinder-shaped chariot was of smooth gleaming metal, like the thin fire-sticks. But it was nearly as wide as the Temple that surrounded it. The top pointed up like a nose and stretched high toward the Heavens, like a tree so tall she could not see the top of it no matter how she craned her neck. She remembered how high the center of the Temple looked when she would gaze up at it from far away on the beach. Yes, it was as Melina had once told her. "Many lives ago," she had said, her gentle fingers combing through Sarai's unruly black hair, "the Gods came down to Earth in this, the biggest of their chariots. The gleaming chariot's roaring fires settled it on the wide plateau a-top the high hill and the Gods built their great stone Temple around it."

Sarai stretched out her legs, then crossed them again. She had *watched* the Gods throughout the night, but she could not *see* where they stored their fire-sticks. Each God kept a weapon with him while he worked. Before he retired to sleep in his own large chamber, each God handed his fire-stick to the God he went to rouse. Only a few Gods slept at a time and only for part of the night.

Perplexed, Sarai knit her brows. Why were the Gods not sleeping? Why did each one hold a weapon wherever he went? How could she sneak into the inner chambers to get a fire-stick when the Masters were all about and would see her? Were they so different than the people of Earth that they did not sleep the night through?

She pictured the Temple priestesses and servants in her mind, so innocent in sleep, trusting the Gods who cared nothing for them. Someone—no, probably several of the older menservants— would be snoring now. A priestess might wake and sit up, un- comfortable among so many when she was accustomed to sleeping alone. But the children slept through the night, their breath soft against their sleeping pallets. There were only two small children now at the Temple, brother and sister, gifted to the Gods by their father in the city below the hill. He was too poor to provide for any more children when they were born. He trusted them, Tam and N'Amah, to the great Gods. But the Gods had all but forgotten the babes. It was the people of the Temple who fed them, clothed them, held them, kept them safe.

Thinking of the sleeping little ones, Sarai lay down, too weary to *listen* to the Masters any longer. Her eyelids closed as she vowed, *I will learn what I need to know as soon as I wake.*

"Sarai. Sarai! Are you dead?"

She swam out of sleep. She felt her teeth rattle, shaking along with her head against her sleeping pallet. Elia was clutching Sarai's shoulders, the smaller priestess leaning over her, shaking her. Tears plopped down on Sarai's face.

Sarai squirmed from her grasp and sat up. "Rest yourself, Elia. You can see I am alive."

Elia released her but remained kneeling by her side. "Oooh," she whimpered, wringing her hands. "I thought our God Scrae-Lon had come for you in the night and... and punished you and— killed you! Your face, it's... it's big and—purple!"

The storm pummeled the stones above them. Sarai heard the small window tapestry flapping against the harsh wind. *Elia, Elia,* she thought, *I'd like to throttle you!* But she must keep her patience with the child-like priestess; she acted out of love and concern.

Yes, her head ached, the flesh of her face stung. She remembered the furious God striking her, the force of his blow. Her heart pounded in her throat, but she gathered herself to calm Elia.

"Elia, he did not come for me in the night. I only hope he beat me enough yesterday to satisfy his anger. Please. Stop worrying about me! I am well. I—I have things I must do. I will go with you to take the morning meal."

Elia wiped tears from her eyes with the back of her hand. "Oh I'm glad, Sarai," she sniffled. "Come. It's late."

Scrae-Lon did not call for Sarai as she hurriedly ate her morning meal, nor did he come for her throughout the day while she sat alone in her alcove, *listening* to them. None of the Gods appeared outside the inner chambers. They ignored all the priestesses, all the servants.

Over the drumming of the ceaseless rain, no one heard anything of the Gods until A-Don came into the hearth hall during the evening meal. Like the other Gods, he held his gleaming metal fire-stick in one hand. "Remove the things you have brought into the hall," he commanded. "Then bring food for your Gods,"— here he pointed his long fire-stick at the far wall across from the hearth—"and leave it by that wall. Bring food for three meals and do not enter this hall until next evening, when you will again bring food for us. Go! Do as I bid you."

Sarai understood little of what she *heard* during the day, but she stayed in her alcove and persisted in *listening*. Before the time of the evening meal, she *saw* several Gods—Run-Gon, Lew-Ron, Bin-Duss and Jor-Gum among them—come through the back entrance of the Temple to the landing platform. Each wore the same black cloak, shirt, trousers and boots that she had seen Z'Shar wearing and each God still carried a fire-stick. She realized the black suits protected them from the wind and rain. They watched as a round chariot settled to the ground on its roaring orange and blue fires.

When the flames were gone, a door-like opening appeared on the side of the chariot that faced the Temple. Four other Gods, all clad in black suits, stepped onto the landing platform and greeted the Temple Masters. Then she *saw* many metal containers, some small but mostly large, wider than the breadth of a God's arms, come floating out of the Temple! As though they were alive and could fly like birds, the metallic objects floated to the doorway of the resting chariot and disappeared inside. One after another they came, like ants following each other on an ant trail high above the ground.

Finally, the last metal box drifted through the opening. The black-cloaked Gods—except for Jor-Gum—followed, walking through the rain until they too disappeared into the resting chariot. The fat God went back into the Temple and moments later came out again with Scrae-Lon. Sarai stiffened when she *saw* her adversary, but never wavered from *watching*. After the two remaining Gods went into the chariot, the doorway hissed closed behind them. Soon the chariot belched the familiar blue and orange flames and rose into the storming skies.

Scrae-Lon had gone to the skies! Sarai fell back on her sleeping pallet, laughing and crying. Although she had not *heard* any of the Masters speak of her disobedience or how she would be punished, it was still a relief that Scrae-Lon was gone. She joined the other Temple folk for the evening meal, ate at her leisure and enjoyed the company, especially when she played with the two children. Later, A-Don entered the hearth hall and, like the other respectful people of the Temple, Sarai hastened to leave and obey his commands.

Although she had slept very little the previous night, she meant to sit up in her alcove *listening* again this night. But now her belly was full and it felt good to lie down and close her eyes in the darkness of the storm. The exhausted priestess drew a deep breath, felt her breast rise and fall against her sleeping pallet. She did not *hear* the Gods. She slept.

EIGHT

Flashes of unworldly light and demonic answering thunder woke her several times during the night, but she was exhausted and fell quickly back to sleep. Towards morning she slept soundly, until her *hearing* startled her awake. She jerked upright, her eyes wide and staring.

Scrae-Lon had returned. Inside her head, she *saw* him and three other Gods she did not recognize by the landing platform at the back of the Temple. Once again, metal objects floated through the air, parading one after the other through the dark opening into the resting chariot. After the last object disappeared through the doorway, Scrae-Lon moved back to the Temple walls and watched the other Gods go through the chariot door. The roaring chariot rose into the dark clouds.

Scrae-Lon strode back through the Temple. Sarai gulped. She could not *see* where he went.

The howling, crashing storm forced her thoughts back to her surroundings. Only gray light filtered in through the cold, stone walls. Rolling, roaring thunder, as loud as the Gods' fire-belching chariots, shook the ground beneath her. The little tapestry covering the opening in the rock flapped in the wind, showering her with droplets of water. Rainwater puddled beneath the window and seeped onto one side of her sleeping pallet and thin blanket. Her thin sleeping shift felt damp. She sprang up and dragged her pallet next to the entrance to her alcove then pulled off her shift and searched out a dry tunic.

Cries and shouts rang out. She hurried after two servants who ran to the steps at the Temple entrance. There, hoards of bedraggled people beseeched the Gods to give them shelter inside the Temple. "The city is flooded," some of them cried, "and we are forced to flee our homes!" Others, terrified, shouted that their flimsy huts had collapsed and floated away in the rising waters. Would the terrible storm never end? "Great powerful Gods!" they pleaded, "Help us! We will surely die!"

Scrae-Lon, still clad in his black suit, stood with Sh'Baal at the top of the staircase. Shaking their heads at the people's desperate cries, they said nothing, but kept their fire-sticks pointed into the midst of the surging crowd.

Dressed in rich ceremonial robes, A-Don appeared behind them, holding his large metal speaking cup over his mouth. "Go!" the tallest, red-haired God commanded the terrified people. "There is no room for you here. Go higher, into the hills. There you will be safe."

Sarai cringed. She knew he was lying to them. But the people trusted their most powerful God and a good many of them turned to trek through the Temple grounds toward the even higher hills that led to the mountains. Many dragged wailing children by the arms. They carried nothing but the wet clothing on their backs for the rain had taken everything else.

Tasting the bile rising in her throat, Sarai tightened her hands into fists. The Masters would do nothing to save the people. A-Don had sent them fleeing faster to their deaths. She wanted to strangle him and crush his pink face under the heavy speaking cup.

She tore her eyes from the struggling crowds and looked out beyond to the distant sea. She gasped. It seemed as though the sea had opened its mouth to swallow the city. High, crashing waves hurled themselves over the beach. Marusha's old hut and others nearby were mere straw caught in the tumbling waters. Like logs of flesh, the helpless people perished and were rolled before the wind and waves. The city was drowning.

Loud sobbing welled up behind her. She turned around and joined the heart-broken group of priestesses and Temple servants. They shivered in the wind and clutched at each other, crying louder in their desperation. They were powerless to help the drowning, dying people. They dared not defy their fire-stick-wielding Masters.

A-Don broke into the group, thrusting several servants aside with his powerful arms as if they were mere bundles of fodder. Most of the wailing ceased as the remaining servants and priestesses knelt to the wet ground before their God.

"Rise!" he commanded. "Get thee away from the entrance."

They scrambled to obey and he followed them with long strides. "Stop!" he ordered when they were well inside the Temple.

59

Most still held tightly to each other, some grasping hands, others with arms wrapped about each other, hugging close. Sarai had locked elbows with Elia, but glowering intently she looked straight at A-Don. *I will kill you! I will find the way.*

A-Don whirled about and glared behind as though he had *heard* her. Seeing no threat, he turned back to face his trembling slaves. "Listen to me!" he shouted over the storm. "We Gods know that the storm will not stop; there will be more flooding. We must leave you soon and go to rest in other Temples in the skies above. You are free to go to safety with the other people. Find your families! Go with them to the higher hills. Go until you reach the mountains. You will be safe."

Sarai choked with fury. She knew he lied, but she could never convince the others. They were already dispersing, many running to gather a few precious possessions or their remaining dry clothing. In this storm, a warm cloak was gold; few had them in this mild, coastal climate.

Elia tugged at her arm. "Sarai, come with us! My brother, his wives and family are still here, waiting."

Coming back to herself, Sarai looked into the frightened eyes of the other priestess and shook her head. "Go, Elia!" she urged her companion. "Go swiftly! I will follow soon. I will find you."

"But Sarai," Elia pleaded, "I am afraid for you. There is no time. You must not be alone. Please, come with us now!"

Sarai bent and gently embraced the smaller woman. "Elia, you go. Go with your family. I will be all right. I promise to find you."

Smiling through her tears, she released Elia and stepped back.

She was ashamed that she lied. Poor Elia loved her, trusted her and was ready to adopt Sarai into her own family. It was useless to tell her that the Gods had deceived everyone. Elia would praise the Gods with her final words and love them with her last breath. She and her brother would never be able to climb high enough into the hills to escape the flood. No one would. Only the Gods in their fiery sky chariots could outrun the waters that rose to swallow the Earth.

Weeping, Elia turned and joined her waiting family, shivering in the rain at the foot of the steps. Wiping away her own tears, Sarai drew breath and headed back into the Temple. In the little time left, her purpose was clear: kill every God she could find.

Scattered *voices* of the Gods cascaded between her ears. The last of them planned to abandon the Temple and leave together in the great sky chariot. She needed to be alone, to think, to plan quickly. Scrae-Lon and Sh'Baal must not see her when they came back through the Temple. Where could she go? Yes! The children's room. It would be empty and no one would think to look for her there. She dashed through the Temple towards her destination, unnoticed by person or God.

Panting, she flung herself onto one of the sleeping pallets. It was soaked, so she moved to another, closer to the entrance of the small alcove. Thunder rumbled. Someone screamed. Furious rain pelted the Temple, sounding more like thousands of pebbles than the deadly downpour it was.

Suddenly, the ground shook beneath her. Her heart pounded in her throat. She swallowed hard as if to force it back down. The old, ripped hemp cover flew from the doorway as though one of the giant Gods had torn it away. Sarai lay flat on her belly, hands covering her head. The stone walls groaned against the torrents of rain. Thunder roaring, the storm thrust its mighty fist against the Temple and burst through the wall!

Sarai sprang up and fled through the rain. Feeling dryer ground beneath her feet she paused, her chest heaving. Her mind *grasped* at the great sky chariot and the Gods waiting beside it. She had to find one of their fire-sticks before she reached the inner chamber. Where were the weapons? She started toward the hearth hall, slowly picking her way through fallen rocks and debris. She would search the forbidden chambers. As the light from outside grew dimmer, she stumbled.

Sarai caught herself and stopped short. She stared down at the fallen God Scrae-Lon lying flat on his back, fainted. Blood dripped in a thin line from his forehead to the ground. He lay next to a collapsed pillar that had broken into two massive stone chunks. There was a gleam of metal—his long fire-stick had rolled a few feet away from his outstretched arm. Sarai pounced on the weapon. Her eager fingers ran over it as she remembered all she had *heard* about how to use it.

The God moaned. Sarai whirled about, weapon poised in her hands. Her nostrils flared. Groaning with the effort, Scrae-Lon slowly pushed himself up till he sat amidst the rubble, legs extended. Glancing up, he sucked in his breath at the sight of Sarai in warrior's stance. She pointed the fire-stick straight between his wide eyes.

"P-priestess," he spluttered. "What are you doing? P-put d-down the weapon!"

She narrowed her eyes.

Scrae-Lon whimpered, "P-please, Sarai! Do not do this. Do not kill your God! I beg you!"

"Don't beg me." She spat. She swallowed, hesitating.

"Please! No." Tears ran down his bloodied face. Weakly he tried to stand, but fell over on his side. He cried out as his head bumped the ground.

She hated him. Hot molten iron flowed through her veins. Now. She must kill him now. She fired the weapon. Scrae-Lon shrieked. Rooted to the ground she stood, undaunted by his screams. Even after the fire had burnt him to ash, the acrid stench of his charred flesh haunted the air like a desolate ghost crying to her about the life she had taken. Still she was unmoved.

"Sarai! What have you done?"

Z'Shar stood on the other side of the silent ashes. She had not heard him come. He leapt beside her and reached for the gleaming weapon, but she clutched the fire-stick next to her breast and ran until a huge pile of rubble blocked her path. She turned and pointed the fire-stick at Z'Shar.

"Leave me alone!" she screamed, her eyes flashing like the lightning of the storm. "You know I know how to use this."

Z'Shar stopped several feet from her. His face was pale, pinched. "Sarai, you don't have to do this," he choked out. "They are all leaving. The Temple is falling in the rain and the mud. I can take you away. There is a safe place—"

"No!" she shrieked. "You know what they did! They killed—they *murdered* so many people, the people I loved!"

"Sarai—"

"I won't kill you—just go away and let me do what I need to do!"

"Sarai, you are killing your own kind—"

"No!" she screamed. "No, I am not like them."

"Sarai, you *are* like us—you are more like me than any of the people of Earth. You *know* this."

"No!" she screeched above the thunder. "Stop. Let me be. Go away."

Suddenly he was gone. Vanished. Sarai caught her breath and held it, then released it in a groan. Sweat trickled into her eyes and down her cheeks. Trembling, she wondered if she had imagined him there. She clenched her teeth. It didn't matter who she was. She had vowed to kill the Gods she hated. She must kill as many of them as she could find before the storm took her own life.

NINE

Searching around, she spied an opening beside the pile of rocks and rubble. Still clutching the powerful weapon to her breast, she tiptoed on bare feet through the rocks and sand covering the wet floor. Two Gods' *voices* tumbled into her spinning mind. They were standing next to the giant sky chariot in the great inner chamber. She stopped and shook her head, trying to steady the spinning; it didn't help. Lowering her heels to the ground she carefully picked her way through the rubble, following the *voices* without trying to understand the *words* as she made her way to the inner chamber.

"*Where is Scrae-Lon?*" said Sh'Baal. "*Do you think he got hurt? The ground is shaking.*"

"*I doubt it.*" A-Don stretched. "*Are there any earthlings left in the Temple? When we launch the ship it will bring the rest of the hill down even quicker than the storm.*"

"*No way to know. You told them to go. They do what their God tells them. But they'll never reach higher ground—too far.*" He yawned. "*They're all going to die, anyway. This whole planet's drowning.*"

"Yes," sighed A-Don, *"and this is really a beautiful planet. It's sad. All the Earth people will perish."*

"Certainly they will all perish," scoffed Sh'Baal. *"So will all the other animals."*

"You still think of them as animals? You pleasured with the priestesses. We all did."

Sh'Baal scowled. *"I can't explain it. They're not people like we are."*

A-Don raised an eyebrow. *"You've heard the evidence. We share the same seed since our worlds collided eons past—we're just farther along. And bigger. We were once as primitive as they are."*

"Hard to believe. Hey! What—"

Sarai burst into the large chamber brandishing the fire-stick. Now it was *her* weapon.

Shocked, Sh'Baal dropped his jaw and his own fire-stick. But A-Don fired on Sarai's weapon so that it grew white with sudden, intense heat. As the hot metal burned her hands, she screamed and let the fire-stick drop to the stone floor where it rolled and clattered towards the sky chariot. Shaking, Sh'Baal bent to retrieve his fire-stick and both Gods leveled their weapons at Sarai. Her breast heaving, she narrowed her eyes and clenched her fists.

"Priestess, do not move!" commanded A-Don. "What are you doing here? Where did you get the weapon?"

Sarai stood still, silent.

"Answer your God!"

Deliberately, she hawked and spat.

Sh'Baal gnashed his teeth. "Kill her," he urged his leader. "She must have got the weapon from Scrae-Lon. Maybe she killed him."

"Did you kill your God?" A-Don roared at her. "You will die."

"Kill me!" Sarai shrieked, springing at the armed Gods with her hands stretched out like the claws of a wild animal. But before the Gods could fire their deadly weapons, a burst of wind flew between them and Sarai's world went black.

TEN

Sarai awakened feeling nauseous and rolled over on the wet grass. She pushed herself onto her elbows, retched and rolled onto her back. Closing her eyes, she rested prone until her breath came easier. She knew she was outside, far from the Temple and the Gods she wanted to kill. The ceaseless rain pelted down around her, but did not fall on her body. Strange.

She opened her eyes and gazed up at a smooth, gray metal covering extending above her about twice the length of her body. The rain fell in sheets on three sides, but there was a wall of the same smooth metal near her bare feet. Catching her breath, she recognized a sky chariot of the Gods. Z'Shar stood next to it under the gray ceiling, wrapped in his hooded black cloak. She could not see his face, but she knew it was him.

Clenching her jaw she sat up, legs crossed. Glowering at his black hood, she demanded, "Why did you bring me here? I told you to leave me."

Z'Shar lowered his hood with one hand. He nodded, but did not speak aloud. *I won't let them kill you. And I will not help you kill the others.*

Sarai squeezed her eyes shut and clapped her hands to her ears although she knew she could not block his *voice*. "Stop it!" she screamed. "Stop this—this thing you do. I don't want to *hear* you."

He was silent until she opened her eyes and glared at him. "As you wish," he said slowly. "But I am sad that you do not want to share our *hearing.*"

She felt an ache in her chest, but shook her head. "Leave me. Let me go do what I must. They don't deserve to live and I—I have nothing to live for—oh!" In sudden anguish, she wrapped her arms around herself and bowed her head to the wet ground, weeping.

He knelt in front of her, waiting until there was a break in her sobs. "Sarai, get up. See where we are. It is too late to do anything. Look."

She lowered her hands and peered into his face through the matted clumps of her long black hair. Looking beyond him, she saw only rain splattering to the ground and pooling in the long grass. Combing her hair off her face with her hands, she got to her feet and ground her toes into the mud. Z'Shar stepped to her side.

She gasped and her jaw dropped. Her guts roiled as her mind reeled, taking in where she was. Z'Shar had brought her far above the city—or where the city once was. Now there was only wild, rolling ocean, spewing huge waves toward the tiny, far-off Temple. Under the waves' onslaught, the hill plateau melted like sand and she watched the remaining bit of rubble that had been her home slide like seashells beneath the swirling waters.

The conquering sea was all around. Its maw opened to swallow the land. Like huge tongues the roaring waves licked at the higher hills, even where she now stood. There was no escape.

Sarai swallowed. *I am all alone,* she thought. *Everyone is dead.*

"No, Sarai," Z'Shar spoke gently at her side, "you are not alone. There are other people of Earth who are alive, in a safe place. Some of them are like you, too."

Sarai jerked her head towards him, her heart pounding in her throat. "What do you mean, they are like me?"

They hear, just as you and I do and they were born on Earth, as you were.

She faced him and spat, "Liar!"

He raised his hands, shook his head. "Sarai, I have no reason to deceive you. You know this. Please stop fighting me. You know I am not like the others. I want to help you, but I won't force you to come with me. If you choose to stay here and watch the flood until you die—and the waters will come here, I know—then I won't stop you. But I don't want you to die. I would not let A-Don and Sh'Baal kill you. So I brought you here."

"But how did you—bring me here? What weapon did you use? I did not want you to take me away!"

Z'Shar shrugged his shoulders. "I know. I brought you here— it is just something I can do. You may be able to learn how—but you don't believe you are like me. Maybe in time…"

"I am *not* like you!" she insisted, although doubts wound through her mind like snakes. And he *knew* her doubts. She could hide nothing from him. So she stared at him, frowning.

Z'Shar paused, a smile playing at his lips as his eyes met hers.

"Sarai," he said, "come with me and meet the ones who are like you. I wanted to bring you to them before, but the others found out who I was and I had to leave quickly. I would have come back for you, even if there had been no flood. You know I am telling you the truth."

He seemed to embrace her with his words. Sarai felt a flush rise into her face. She hung her head, her breath quickening. There was no sense resisting him. She knew he would not harm her. If she was to remain alive, she must stay with him. "I will go with you," she said, although she refused to look at him. "But I want nothing to do with any of your kind."

"As you will it," he returned. "I am glad you will come to the safe place." He stood up. "Come out of the rain," he said. "We have to go there in my—sky chariot. It is far."

He stepped to his chariot and touched the metal wall with his fingertips. Beneath the pattering of the rain came a humming sound and the smooth ceiling above seemed to slide into the side of the chariot. Then an opening appeared, a doorway into the sky chariot. Sarai had seen this doorway appear on other chariots of the Gods, but she had never seen inside. Her heart thudded. If she walked through the opening, would she tumble down into a black abyss?

Z'Shar gently took her hand. "You are safe here. I will take you to the safe place."

She let him lead her to the door. "This place—is it in the sky?"

"No, Sarai, it is on the Earth, but very far from here. You cannot imagine—but you will see."

ELEVEN

She stepped inside to another world. It was dry; dry and round, with gleaming metal surrounding her as if she were inside a huge, hollow metal cylinder. There was nothing of Earth in this strange chariot from the skies. Even the chairs seemed wrong: made of the same hard, gray metal with arms that looked too wide, they lacked the comfort she expected of a chair. Although the craft was more than twice the size of Marusha's old thatched hut, it held only the two alien chairs side by side towards the front, next to an extensive window that spanned the wall from the floor where she stood to high above her head and reached back behind the chairs. Gazing through the open window, she saw the storm sending sheets of rain to drench the Earth's green hills and tall mountains and swell the rising sea. But the rain did not come through the window into the big, round room: some strange, transparent hardness kept the world out.

In front of the two metal chairs stood a long, rectangular metal table, laden with black and gray knobs and countless small coals of red, blue, green, gold—or were they gems that glowed like fire?

Fascinated, Sarai walked hesitantly towards the strangely beautiful array. She waved her hands above the gems of fire, but felt no warmth from them. Tentatively, she extended her finger and touched a round, golden one. It was cool and hard, like the metal floor beneath her muddy feet.

A humming sound brought her attention back to the doorway through which they had entered. Z'Shar had again touched the wall and she watched the opening disappear. Quiet stillness filled her ears. She could not hear the storm. She gasped and stumbled around the gem-studded table, reaching for the rain beyond the window. Even though she expected a barrier, her fingers buckled against the clear, hard material. A knot tightened in her throat. She began to pant. *I cannot get out.*

"I know you are afraid. You have never seen these things. Let me help you." He walked toward her.

"No. Do not—let me be. I can do—I don't know—how can you help me?"

Open to me. I can hear what you need.

"No." She drew a breath. "I don't want to *hear* you. I can't stop you *listening* to me, but I don't want you to touch me—inside. I can—be calm. Only tell me what I need to do to make the journey to where the others are."

He sighed and shrugged his shoulders. "There is not much for you to do. Wait." He turned away and went to the back of the room where there appeared to be a small, walled-off alcove. When he touched the wall another doorway appeared.

He disappeared through the opening and for a moment Sarai

73

feared he had left her alone in the silent metal chariot. But he soon emerged from the darkness, carrying a smooth, square white box and a clear, cylindrical vessel. He touched the wall with his elbow and the opening grew narrower until it was gone.

Returning to her side, he deposited the objects into niches on the wide arm of one of the chairs. Wordlessly, he pointed to the other chair. She padded over to it on her bare feet and sat down on the cold metal. Her wet flesh slid back over the smooth surface. Once she was seated the chair grew soft, cushioning her bottom and her back. And it began to warm her, drying her. Sarai's eyes widened and she stared at Z'Shar seated next to her. He smiled.

"I know this is very strange to you," he said kindly, all the while fingering, pulling, tapping at the smooth knobs and glowing gems on the table in front of his chair. "You will see things you have never imagined. Sarai, trust me. No harm will come to you. As soon as you are safe, you will not have to see me again. But I wish—I wish until then you will be open to me. We can share this journey together, if you will allow it."

"I don't know," she said, squirming in the chair even though it was now so warm and comfortable. "I don't think I have any choice but to share with you. I have no power here."

He let his hands rest on the table and turned his head. His black eyes burned into her. "I have no power over you. You know too well I am not your God."

Her throat tightened and her eyes welled with tears. "You are no God, but you hold my life in your hands."

"You chose to live. You can also choose not to hate me."

"Yes, I can choose."

He stared at her as tears started down her cheeks. She looked down at her hands clasped together in her lap, her fingernails digging into her flesh.

She heard the humming again, but now it grew louder, like an animal growling, until it was a thundering roar. The chariot trembled and shook and then she was shaking inside, as though she had become part of the roaring chariot. There came a pressure over her, as though one of the giant Gods lay upon her, holding her down. She pushed to get out of the chair, but could not move. Helpless, she gave a silent scream.

He was there, *speaking* to her between her ears. *Sarai, the pressure will pass. We are rising off the Earth. Let me help you. Open to me.*

She stared into his face. *Yes.*

Given her consent, he *joined* with her *inner voice* and helped her find what she needed to overcome her fear:

She was a very small child again, nestled in dear Melina's lap. Melina kissed her ear and sang to her as she brushed her tussled black hair. Sarai laughed and twisted around until her little fingers found their way inside one of Melina's long, almond-brown curls.

Then she grew tall and strong. Z'Shar stood next to her, hugged her close, stroking her hair down her back. She breathed in the warm scent of him. "You are safe here," he whispered into her ear.

She was staring into his smiling eyes. With a jolt, she realized they had never left their chairs.

"Better now?"

"Yes, thank you." She paused, dizzy. "I'm not afraid, but the room—it is going around—"

He nodded. "That will pass as the pressure lessens. Take big, slow breaths. Look through the window. You can watch as we rise higher."

Below her, through the heavy rain, the green hills were but rolling knolls next to the tempestuous advancing waters of the sea. In only moments they skimmed the mountaintops. The mountains seemed to flee away behind the chariot. The wondrous sight filled her like pure, sweet air and her mouth opened in a broad smile.

She blinked. It was hard to see through the rain. It had grown fuzzy and white and now all the mountains were covered with white.

"Snow and ice," Z'Shar explained. "Very cold. You have never seen it. You have never felt such cold. It can kill us."

"But it is not cold in here."

He laughed. "No, not inside here. Outside, high in the mountain country, it is colder than you have ever known. But the safe place is in the highest mountain. None of the giant men you hate go there. That is why it is safe."

She frowned. "Are we going inside a mountain? How can it be safe if I will die?"

He shook his head, laughing again. "You know I would not bring you there to die. Many people are living there. The place is protected from the cold. You will see. Do not be afraid. Look outside and see how beautiful the Earth is!"

"Yes," she agreed. Her eyes widened, as though to take in even more of everything she saw. She drew it in and stored these sights in her heart, where she stored similar treasures.

"Are you hungry?"

She gave a start. Yes, she was ravenous; she had not eaten since the previous day. Lowering her gaze to the arm of his chair, she watched Z'Shar lift the flat lid from the white box. He reached over to the arm of her chair and fit the open container into a similar niche. Inside were nuts, peaches, strawberries, bits of carrots and green beans and what appeared to be cut-up cheese. She grabbed a handful of nuts and greedily shoved them into her mouth, swallowing too soon. She choked and coughed, tears running from her eyes.

Z'Shar smiled and handed her the clear vessel, already opened. "It's water," he said. "Hard to believe there is so much water on the Earth right now. Drink. I knew you were hungry. I have plenty of food. Eat as much as you want."

As he spoke, she put the mouth of the strange, smooth vessel to her lips, tipped it up and tentatively tasted the clear liquid. The water was fresh and pure and soothed her throat. She drank deeply and then found a niche for the vessel on the arm of her chair. "Thank you," she said, wiping the tears from her cheeks.

He nodded, smiling again. They were silent while Sarai ate until there was nothing left. She drank more water, set the remainder back into the niche and gazed out the window, rapt at the spectacle of the snow falling to the mountaintops.

Z'Shar reached for the water, tilted his dark head back and

gulped down the rest of it. A short while later, he said, "We will arrive soon. I am lowering the chariot to the Earth. You will feel a little pressure again as we come down to the ground. Nothing to fear."

Sarai took a deep breath, releasing it slowly. The force on her was not great, not unpleasant when she knew what to expect. Through the window, she watched the snow-laden mountains loom taller and taller above and all around them as the craft descended to Earth. It halted with a jolt and then seemed to slide a little over the ground. At length she saw no movement and the humming ceased.

Taking both containers, Z'Shar stood and walked back to the alcove on the opposite side of the chariot. He entered, blocked from her view. Moments later he emerged carrying black clothing like his own, which he handed to her. He set a pair of similar black boots in front of her on the floor.

"Dress in these to keep warm," he instructed. "Your tunic should be dry now. Put this clothing over it. First we must go outside. I cannot move us through the walls of the ship."

"I don't understand," said Sarai, questions tumbling into her mind. "We came in here through that—doorway."

"Yes," he said. "But first I brought you from the Temple to the hills. To my chariot."

"Oh." Sarai remembered rolling over in wet grass. "How did you bring me there? I don't know what happened. I was facing A-Don and Sh'Baal and then I was lying on the ground and I was—sick."

Z'Shar nodded. "You are not accustomed to my—wind. It is how I move us. I will teach you to avoid the sickness. When we go outside, hold close to me and think with all your strength that you are next to me. Think of nothing else. Only that we hold together. Dress now."

She dressed. The clothing looked identical to his. There was even a long, black, hooded cloak to throw around herself. The black cloth felt strange: it was thick and smooth as glazed pottery, but soft and flexible as flower petals. In comparison, her tunic felt rough as tree bark.

Z'Shar pulled the hood of her cloak over her tussled black hair so that it draped over her forehead. "Come," he said, taking her hand in his. He led her to the side of the room, pressed the metal wall with his other hand and the entrance appeared. Tugging firmly at her arm, he took her outside.

White flakes whirled around them and Sarai felt gooseflesh rise all over her body. She gasped as the icy wind struck blows at her. Their tall boots crunched in the thick snow on the ground as they struggled to move away from the silent chariot.

"Take hold of me with both arms!" he shouted through the roar of the wind. "Think only about holding on to me!"

She hugged him tightly, wrapping her arms around his back as he threw his own cloak around them both. His arms reached around her, holding her so tightly that she thought she heard the beating of his heart. The heat of his body seemed to mingle with her own, like warm water bathing her, seeping inside her. She squeezed her eyes shut and thought only of holding him closer and closer.

Abruptly, the wind and snow ceased. It was less cold, but not warm. She opened her eyes under his cloak, but still clung to him.

"You did well, Sarai," he said softly and flung open his cloak. "You are still standing. Do you feel sick?"

"No."

"Good. Then you can let go. Some time, if you wish, I can teach you to use your own wind. Yes, you will learn that you too have a wind. But now, we must walk a little way. You can let go now."

Still she held onto him. She felt him laughing, next to her breast. Reluctantly, she unwound her arms and released him. Stepping back, she eyed her surroundings.

They were in an enormous cavern, so high that she could barely see the top of it. Dark rock surrounded them, covering the domed ceiling, the rough walls and the ground beneath their boots. She remembered him saying the safe place was inside a mountain. Turning around, she spied the opening to the cavern a short distance behind them. Outside, the snow still swirled in the howling wind. The cold crept into the hollow of the mountain, chilling her despite her black coverings. It would be warmer if they followed the cavern deeper inside. It frightened her to think of going deep within the mountain, but she did want to get warm.

"Come," Z'Shar urged and continued talking as they pressed forward, following the twists and turns of the wide cavern. "I will bring you to the people and then I must go quickly. I want to search for others who may still live."

"Other people who *hear*?"

"Anyone—and animals, too. I'm afraid I will be too late. I stayed a long time with you, hoping you would come with me. I would not force you to come with me. You were stubborn with anger."

Her stomach turned over. Full of remorse, she thought perhaps other people could have lived but for her pride and rage.

You didn't know, Z'Shar *said* gently. *There was no way for you to know.*

"But—I am so sorry!" she cried, running to keep up with his long strides.

"I know," he said over his shoulder. "Here, take my hand."

She reached for his hand and as if she were a small child he pulled her with him.

TWELVE

Around a bend, they suddenly came to a much wider and taller area of the cavern. One side of this enormous space was completely transparent, a giant window like the one in Z'Shar's sky chariot. Squinting through the window into the grayness of the storm, Sarai saw a wide valley spreading out below the mountains. She could barely make out the tops of huge stone buildings almost buried in the snow and many tall, massive trees, bending like twigs in the brutal wind.

She brought her gaze back to the cavern. Opposite the window, the inner side was filled with alcoves covered by skins and furs, and stone fireplace niches where huge fires burned, sending glowing warmth and light into the spacious cavern. The smoke rose through holes in the rock above. Clothed in heavy furs, a short, dark-skinned man tended the closest fire, but he turned and cried out when Z'Shar and Sarai arrived. Then she saw many excited others, men and women and a few young ones. Some people came from the alcoves, some ran towards them from further back in the cavern. Most looked similar to the fire tender, with short, muscular, fleshy bodies and dark eyes and hair. She also noticed with some surprise that most of the men had no beards, or wore just a little wispy facial hair. Many people wore furs, but others were clothed in smooth black fittings such as she and Z'Shar wore.

"Z'Shar! Z'Shar!" they called. Those who reached him first fell upon him with embraces and spoke joyfully in words Sarai could not understand. As the people surrounded him she let go of his hand, but stayed close, shy among the strangers. Z'Shar towered over them and smiled into their upturned faces. When he spoke to them in their language she could understand, for she could *hear* his meaning.

"I have brought another woman to you," he said as he leaned down to hug the people surrounding him. "Take good care of her, show her your ways. Those of you who are Listeners must teach her your language. I am sorry, but I must leave you now. I go to search for others who still live through the storms."

Sarai *heard* a *voice, two voices, three, four.* They *greeted* her warmly. Looking out among the crowd, she spied three taller people and a growing child. A man and a woman standing together, holding the child in front of them, looked like the other short, dark-haired, sparse-haired people. There was also a big man with skin even darker, a deep rich brown the color of his dark eyes. He held the hand of one of the smaller women who was big with child, obviously his mate, who had no inner voice. Sarai knew these were the ones like her, the others Z'Shar had told her about, born on Earth with the *hearing.* Brimming with happiness at meeting them, she *shouted* back her own joyful *greetings*. She waved her arms in wide circles, mirroring her inner excitement.

Zillah! Zillah! My beloved daughter!

The *voice* burst into her head and moments later she saw a bald-headed old man run from behind the crowd, pushing people to the side as he made his way towards Sarai. His eyes were lit and his mouth opened in a joyful smile. He stumbled, caught himself and pressed forward. But he halted a few paces before her, his outstretched arms falling dejectedly to his sides, his mouth slack. Tears formed in his blue eyes. "You are not Zillah," he mourned aloud, in Sarai's native tongue. "You are too big. But— you, you look so much like my daughter! I thought Z'Shar had brought my Zillah to me."

Sarai quickly looked for Z'Shar, but did not see his head above the others. Out of the corner of her eye, she saw the taller couple approaching with their child, still *sending* her their *greetings*. But she was most fascinated by the old man and stared at him. With a little cry, she realized who he was. "I—I know you!" she exclaimed. "You speak my language and I have seen you before, in the city where I lived."

"Are you one of them, the giants from the skies? I have seen only one of the women."

"No!" Sarai was vehement. "I am *not* one of them. I was their—servant—when I saw you. I was a little girl and I saw you confront the false Gods. I knew you spoke the truth!"

"You were there that day," he breathed. He stepped toward her, firm of foot, his shoulders held square. He was nearly as tall as she and looked her directly in the eye, though he squinted when he was close to her. She waited while he studied her. He blinked, rubbed his eyes and stepped back.

"I saw you escape them," Sarai continued. "Everyone else ran away as A-Don commanded, but I hid from them and I watched and I know they did not burn you with the fire-stick! How did you get away? How did you come here?"

"Z'Shar brought me here, just as he has brought you," he explained. "He took me away in his wind and brought me here in his sky chariot and I have been here ever since. I am glad you have come to us. It is very good to hear the tongue of my birth. I am Mendano. What are you called?"

"Sarai," she answered. "I never forgot you since the day I saw you. I thought often about what you said. May I—may I come close to you? May I hold your hands in mine?"

"Yes, child. Child? You are so big, like one of them."

"I *hate* them!" Sarai insisted. "I am not one of them!" She took his large hands in hers.

Mendano squinted as he peered at her. "Ah, yes, I understand you hate them," he murmured.

Closing his eyes into his own thoughts, he turned his face to the ground. Then he looked back into her face, squinting again. He sighed and said quietly, "My eyes, they sometimes deceive me when I look too close. But you do look so much like my daughter." He smiled at the memory. "Your eyes—they could be her eyes. You are dark like she was, too. She looked so much like her mother."

His eyes welled with tears and his voice rose. "My poor Tamar, she died giving birth. Perhaps Zillah was too big for her... That made the giants want her. They raped my daughter, those monsters from the skies! Two of them grabbed her and took her and a third held me so I couldn't stop them. I thought she would die the way she screamed!"

He paused as more tears rolled down his cheeks. "But she lived and bore a child—a girl. I told her to kill the little monster! But she ran away from me with it and when she returned she said she had brought her child to a safe place. I suppose," he sighed, "I suppose a mother feels differently, after carrying a child for all those months, even if the father is one of the giants. My own mother told me I was also a child of the Gods. She was honored to serve the Gods when they wanted her. " He spat to the side. "They're monsters! I spoke out to the people of our city because I wanted them to know those monsters are not Gods. I knew they would kill me, but I didn't care.

"But Z'Shar, he is different. I would be dead but for him. And now he has also brought you here, Sarai. It is so good to talk with someone from my home." He stepped back again, eyeing her up and down. "It's amazing." He slowly shook his pink head and stepped back further. "You look so much like my daughter, but you are the tallest woman of Earth that I have ever seen! I wonder if you got that from the giants, as I did."

Sarai wept silently. The old man stepped close to her and took her hand. Still staring at him, she said, "I think—oh, I believe I am your grand-daughter. I was left at the Temple as a tiny baby.

No one ever knew where I came from. And you know—I can *hear* them—the giants, the way Z'Shar *hears* them. I can *hear* you, too, though maybe not as well as I *hear* the giant men. I—I am so happy to see you!"

Smiling, he took her into his arms and embraced her. Sarai mumbled into his shoulder, "I have been so angry." She raised her head and looked into his bearded face. "Z'Shar, he came for me and took me away from there to bring me here. He knew I was like him, but I refused to believe it. If you are my grandfather then there is more monster in me than Earth woman!" She buried her face in his shoulder and began to sob.

Mendano stroked her hair with one hand. "Sarai, Sarai," he soothed, "you are no monster, dear child. I need only look at you, listen to you and hold you next to me to know there is more of Zillah in you than any giant from the skies. You must not hate who you are. I am also happy you are here with me."

Sarai hugged him again. Then she released him and looked for Z'Shar. "Where is Z'Shar?" she wondered aloud. "I—I want to tell him how sorry I am. I want to tell him how grateful I am for all he has done for me."

Z'Shar has gone, said the tall, darkest man. *He searches for others in the storm.*

"No!" wailed Sarai. "Oh no!" She looked into the faces of the tall ones who stood near her, the ones she knew could *hear* her. *Will he return soon?*

He will return, but it may be a long time, answered the tall woman with the *hearing*. *Or perhaps he will return sooner, but usually he is gone long. We don't know where he goes, but he always comes back to us.*

"Then he will believe I hate him all the time he is gone," Sarai mourned aloud. She covered her face with her hands and wept. Mendano gently embraced her, but she would not be comforted.

THIRTEEN

While the unrelenting snows fell on the mountains and in the valleys, Sarai lived with Mendano, her grandfather, sharing his alcove in the cavern high up within the ancient mountain. For the first time since she could remember she had a family, even if it was just the two of them. Perhaps because they were only two, she usually called him "Grandfather Mendano." She wanted to stretch out the sounds of their blood ties, as though she were singing a song with many verses about her family. Together, they found comfort as they mourned those they had known and lost in the city of their birth.

She remained determined to make amends with Z'Shar whenever he returned, for she was deeply grateful to him for bringing her to this safe place. She had found her happiness in her unique new home. She belonged with Grandfather Mendano and the other people who had come together from so many different places.

Although his wrinkled, bald head and long white beard revealed his age, Grandfather was strong and sure-footed as an old mountain goat. Under his tutelage, she learned the ways of the mountain family. He taught her to tend the fires of the cavern. He showed her how the people stored their food where it was colder, close to the wide entrance to the cavern on the far, other side of the mountain. The place for waste and washing was near the outer hearth, on the side where she and Z'Shar had entered, before the wide window began.

Since Grandfather Mendano was often frustrated when he could not see well close up, Sarai soon convinced him to allow her to take over his part in preparing the meals that the small community shared in the widest part of their protected domain within the mountain. But most of the day, the family of two walked back and forth through the cavern, talking in their native tongue, sharing many years of thoughts, memories and inspirations. Passersby enjoyed the alien music of their foreign language.

Between the hushed blackness of each night, only dim gray light marked each day. After she woke in the mornings, Sarai cleaned and tidied the small alcove in which they slept. It was second nature to her, for she had grown up as a servant in the Gods' Temple. She found a straw broom for sweeping, old rags for scrubbing and a bucket for water. There was, after all, plenty of water; she only needed to gather up the piling snow at either end of the cavern and bring it inside to melt. There was always water boiling and steaming in dark earthen pots suspended over the fires in the hearths.

Every time she cleaned, Grandfather smiled and rolled his eyes. "I thank you," he chuckled, "but why work so hard? These old eyes don't notice the dirt." However, the first time he saw her stoop to lift the vessel where he made his waste during the night, intending to bring it to the area where she could cover it with ash, Grandfather laughed and put his hand over hers. "Stop, Sarai," he said. "You have done enough. This I can do for myself."

His gratitude was unfamiliar to her, for she knew no other life besides one of unquestioned servitude. She had much to learn. Within the mountain, beneath the layers of rock, her horizons were expanding in unimagined directions.

Sweet as it was to be with her grandfather, Sarai felt added joy to be with Mar, Roe, Crue and Ariza, who were Listeners like her. Aside from Z'Shar, she had never known they existed. They were her people, her tribe, and she would always be with them. Through sharing their *hearing*, they quickly taught her the common language of the dark-eyed cavern-dwellers. Learning and understanding came so swiftly with the *hearing* that sometimes she felt dizzy. She was not used to her own inner voice. The others laughed and suggested that when she felt overcome they could all speak aloud; thus she would learn faster to speak to everyone in the cavern. They were her teachers.

Like Sarai, the other Listeners had grown up far away from each other and never dreamed there were others until Z'Shar brought them together. Only Mar had grown up in the little mountain community that survived each winter in the great cavern. He was the first to tell his story.

FOURTEEN

One morning soon after she arrived, Sarai sat cross-legged before the vast cavern window, her nose nearly touching the strange, clear barrier that separated her from the swirling white world outside. All she could see was a sea of snow flurries, as though she were suspended in a bubble in the midst of it.

An empty bucket rested in her lap. After sweeping out the alcove she shared with Grandfather Mendano, she had attempted to wash the black clothes that Z'Shar had given her, which she had worn for a few days. They were warm and comfortable and she supposed that was why many of the cavern-dwellers wore identical clothing.

In front of their alcove, which was near a glowing hearth, she had knelt on a fur and pushed the smooth black shirt and trousers into the bucket filled with water warmed by the fire. After rubbing them under the water, she lifted the garments from the bucket. To her surprise, all the water ran off the bundle within moments, into the bucket and onto the ground next to the alcove. The clothes felt warm and dry. She sniffed them, as a dog would: they had no odor, no fragrance. With a shrug, she stood and dropped the fur she wore to the ground. She pulled the dry shirt down over her chest and gratefully stepped into the warm trousers. After emptying the bucket in the washing area, she paused to rest and stare through the window.

"Hello Sarai," Mar greeted her.

Lost in her bubble floating in the snow, she had not heard him arrive. She jumped up so she could talk to him face-to-face. Of all the men she had encountered, Mar was the only man of the Earth as tall as her. She enjoyed looking straight into his slanted brown eyes. She noted again that like most of the men living in the warm cavern, he had no beard or other facial hair, other than his thin eyelashes and eyebrows.

He was quick to *hear* her delight. "I too am glad you are as tall as I," he said aloud. "I get lonely up here. Come, I'll sit with you." They sat down side by side in front of the window and he crossed his legs as she did. "Let's try to keep speaking aloud. You are learning so fast. Is there something I can tell you about today?"

"You told me you have always lived here."

"Yes."

"Then how is it that you are taller than the rest of your people? Why are none of them Listeners? Why are your people here where it is so cold?"

"Of course—you do not know. The giants brought us here, long ago, before my grandfather's grandfather lived."

He explained that the giants who called themselves Gods had come to this place and used their machines and weapons to carve the huge shelter into the top of the high mountain. Here they housed themselves, their possessions and their sky chariots, the ships that travelled from star to star in the endless skies above. To serve them in this remote and harshly cold place, the Gods transported a few people of the Earth from the lower lands next to the mountains. When it was warm enough for the snows to melt, the Gods again used their weapons and machines to build massive stone Temples, where the people of Earth served them. Now the people of the mountains still lived in the Temples when it was warm enough, although the Gods had long since abandoned them.

"My people say that not even when they took our women for their own pleasuring did they think of us as more than their slaves, their animals," said Mar, contempt in his voice. Sarai was quick to understand that the people of the mountains knew well that the giant men from the skies were no gods.

Mar continued, "When they decided to go to another place, they took everything they had brought with them—food, machines, rich clothing—and abandoned the cold, stone buildings and the vast cavern. But they did not truly take everything, for they did not care about the people who had served them—the people they left to survive by themselves. 'We will not destroy the cavern for our ships,' they said, thinking themselves big-hearted. 'The Earth people can stay inside it, so they can live through the snows.'

"I think all the holes for fires were already there, and I believe the giants used our sleeping alcoves to store their weapons and other things. We don't remember what they did. It does not matter. They are gone and we don't have to serve them."

Mar paused, drawing breath. He spoke more slowly. "I was always bigger than everyone else around me. People used to say the giants were in my blood. When my grandmother still lived I sometimes *heard* her, but she could not *hear* me and didn't understand what I tried to tell her. I wanted someone to *hear* me, too! Now I know that there are others with the giants in their blood, like you, Sarai. But before Z'Shar came, I didn't know there were other Listeners.

"I remember when Z'Shar first found us and chose to stay with us. I could *hear* him even though his lips never moved! We thought he was one of the giants and we were afraid they would return and make us their slaves again. He came to us alone, but told us he first came from the skies with the other giants. He did not consider himself Master or God to us. I did not want to trust him, but I could *hear* him and came to know him very well. He is often sad. I don't know why, but I cannot help but *hear* his sorrow. I told the others he was not like the other giants; that he was like me. He understood me as no one else did. I was not alone anymore! You must know what that is like."

"Yes, I know." Sarai nodded.

But she was sad and Mar seemed to *know* how she felt. He laid his hand on her shoulder. *Sad Sarai*, he *said, Maybe he is sad the way you are sad. Do not worry. He will return and you can tell him you misunderstood his ways. He knows.*

Sarai tried to smile. Mar spoke aloud again. "I know he cares very much for you, because he trusted us to teach and care for you until he could return. I remember he knew how lonely I felt, with no one else here like me. Soon after he first came, he brought Roe to us—to me. She came from another land far away, where the snows fall thick and heavy as they do here. At last, we had each other! Both of us were Listeners. And we are happy, so happy to be with someone of our own kind."

"I am happy, too!" laughed Crue, his son. Surprised, Sarai smiled at the lithe, black-eyed boy. She had been so engrossed in Mar's words that she did not see the child come up behind them.

She guessed Crue had seen about eight winters. He was tall like his father, with long, straight black hair and his mother's round, sparkling eyes. The boy bent to hug his father and then hugged Sarai. Hugging said what he wanted to say far better than words could.

Crue said he was hungry. Realizing that she had not yet eaten her morning meal, Sarai accompanied them to the central eating area, across from the alcove where she and Grandfather slept. Her kinsman had explained he had chosen his alcove in this warmest area of the cavern, "to keep the cold from creeping into my bones when I sleep." They found him sitting on the ground before the long, low table, feasting on pumpkin seeds, almonds, walnuts and apples. They joined him. Sarai sat beside him, snuggling up next to his black clothing topped by a worn fur. He always wore both; he had never grown used to the mountain winters.

Later in the gray day, she found Ariza stoking a fire that had gone low in the hearth. He was the Listener with deep brown skin nearly as dark as his eyes. He stood to greet her. He was not as tall as Mar, but broader of shoulder, with bulging thighs that made her think longingly of Z'Shar. *If only he would return and hold me close again, touch my secret places…* Oh! Blushing, she tried to push her desire from her thoughts, but part of her still clung to him.

Ariza grinned at her, showing a mouth full of long white teeth. "We cannot hide these feelings from each other," he said. "I hope Z'Shar will return for you soon."

Sarai shook her head. "You don't know. I was—hateful to him."

He winked at her. "You are not hateful now. If I know you want him, then certainly he knows. He will return for you. You are more like him than we are."

She sighed. "I didn't know that until he was gone." She wanted to think about other things, so she asked, "Will you tell me how you came here? Didn't Z'Shar also bring you here?"

"Yes." He took her hand. "Come with me. There is another fire I want to check. That is my favorite task. We can talk more as we walk." He paused, took a breath. "I have only been here for two snow seasons and I still cannot believe the cold. I come from a land where it never snows, where the sun burns most of the days like the fires in this cavern. Oh, how I miss my old home!"

"But you stayed here," said Sarai, keeping step with him.

"Yes," he said softly and Sarai *heard* him remembering his sadness. "There were no other Listeners in my land. I felt so different. People were afraid of me, because I knew things about them. I could *hear* some of the people, the ones who were tall like me, the way all of us sometimes *hear* Mendano."

"I *hear* him almost every day, but he does not *hear* me," Sarai said.

"Yes, that is the way it was for me," continued Ariza. "But Mendano does not fear your *hearing*."

"Before I left the Temple in my city, I *heard* the giants talking about Z'Shar," said Sarai. "I think they were also afraid of him and other Listeners. They hated him and all the others like him. They talked on and on about it."

"So you might understand why I do not return to the land of my birth. I was hated, too. Even my mother was afraid of me. I was hungry for a woman, a mate, but no woman would let me touch her. How lonely I was!

"And then one day, I was walking alone in the jungle as I did most days, I came to the end of the bush, to the low grass and found Z'Shar there, with his strange boat that flies through the skies. I had never seen anything like it and my thoughts were filled with wonder. Z'Shar *spoke* to me right away and when I *heard* him—I think that was the first time I felt truly happy. I think he was just sitting outside his boat *listening* for me, or for anyone who could *hear*. He *told* me he traveled the Earth in search of others like us."

"Yes, that is what he told me, too," nodded Sarai.

"I never even went back to my people." Ariza shrugged his broad shoulders. "I stepped into the sky boat and he brought me here. It was so different! Here no one fears me because I *hear*. And I found Shanga, the woman I love. Soon we will have a child, too. She's sleeping again. I want to check on her, after I fix this fire."

They had reached the other hearth. They knelt down and Sarai helped him with his favorite task.

FIFTEEN

The next day, following the morning meal, Sarai cracked walnuts with Roe and Crue. Using large stones, they pummeled the nuts on a cleaned section of the hard cavern floor until the shells split, depositing the sweet nuts into a large clay bowl.

Crue soon tired of cracking walnuts and invented a game to play. Sitting with his legs apart on the smooth rock ground, he lined up six round nuts in front of him and spun each one with his fingers, trying to get them all spinning at once. The shells were not smooth and the nuts kept coming to rest before he could get to them all. But he was determined to succeed; he did not tire of his game.

"Roe," said Sarai, practicing her new language skills aloud, "how did you decide to come here? I would really like to hear about it."

Roe carefully set her rock on the ground. She smiled at Sarai, crinkling her sparkling black eyes. "I would love to tell you all about it," she said, combing her fingers through the thick black curls of her hair. "I'm glad you are here, Sarai. It has been a long time since I have known another woman Listener."

"You are the only one I have ever known."

"Then we are very important to each other. You see, I grew up with my grandmother, who was a strong Listener. She also healed the sick, because she could somehow *hear* how they hurt, what they needed, so she could help them. Everyone loved her and came to her for advice. They just loved to talk to her. Of course, I was the only one who could *hear* her, although it was hard for me to *hear* anyone else. Even my mother—sometimes I could *hear* her, but she couldn't *hear* me, even though I kept *calling* and *calling* to her."

"Like Grandfather Mendano," said Sarai. "I *hear* him every day, but he does not *hear* me."

Roe took her hand, squeezed it. "Sarai, I think you are a strong Listener, like my grandmother."

"But I don't heal anyone."

Roe smiled again. "There are many ways to heal. You have done much for Mendano."

"Mama! Sarai! Look!"

The women were quick to witness six walnuts spinning at once. "Wonderful!" Roe congratulated the beaming boy, though the spinning shells had already settled still on the ground.

"You did it!" Sarai smiled and clapped her hands.

"I did it," said Crue, jumping to his feet. "I see Tayko. I'm going to play with him." Away he trotted.

I'll hug you later, Roe *told* him.

Sarai shifted, crossing her legs on the ground. Picking up her rock with both hands, she brought it down and cracked the nut with one blow. As she pulled the nutmeat from the shell, she said, "Roe, you seem to know things. You are—wise."

"Me, a Wise Woman." Roe laughed softly. She set down her stone and stretched out her legs. "In my village, everyone expected me to follow my grandmother, to be the Wise Healer when she passed on. I couldn't."

"Why?"

Roe sighed. "Grandmother lived many years, longer than most people in our village ever lived. But her time came. She was not sick, just very old. She died in her sleep. I expected I would be very sad when she left us, but I never thought how much I would hurt. Suddenly, there was no other inner voice in my life. I felt so lost, so alone! I tried to tell people how I felt, but they didn't understand. They weren't Listeners.

"But since I was very small, I had *listened* to the giants when they came to our village, although none of them ever *heard* me when I tried *talking* to them. They came in their sky chariots, because the village was high in the mountains, maybe as high as where we live here. The snows here are no different than they were in my village. We also stayed in caves during the winter, although none of them was near the size of this one. Maybe— maybe my people were high enough on the mountains to escape the flooding from this early winter storm—I don't know. I will ask Z'Shar when he returns."

"Oh Roe, I hope they are alive and safe! It must have been so hard to leave them to come here."

"Yes, I was going to tell you why I left to come here. It had to do with the giants. Like the people in your city, my people thought the giants were gods. They brought them food and gifts and did whatever they asked. They even called for our women to pleasure them and many women were happy to please these self-named Gods. But I stayed away from them. I didn't like them! Their thoughts were so strange and—ugly. I *heard* them. They didn't care about us. They thought we were like animals."

"I know. I *heard* them, too."

"I was always glad they never stayed longer than a few days. I did understand it was too cold for them high up in our mountains.

"Meanwhile I got older, but I never stopped feeling sad about Grandmother. People began to come to me as they had to her, to talk, to get advice and help. But I couldn't help them. I was too sad and lonely. I felt I was failing her. She had also counseled me to follow her path.

"And it was time for me to choose a mate. Sarai, I cannot tell you how much I wanted a mate! Every morning I woke, wishing a man lay sleeping next to me who would wake and touch me, hold me and pleasure me. But I couldn't bear to bond with any man who could not *hear* me."

"Z'Shar must have found you."

Roe nodded. "Yes. I remember it was almost winter when he came. At first I ignored the roar of the sky chariot coming to the ground. I didn't want to *listen* to the giants and their strange, ugly thoughts. But then I *heard* Z'Shar *calling* to anyone who could *hear* him and I *answered* him before I even thought about what I was doing. I was already running towards his sky chariot and he came towards me, too. *'You are lonely,'* he *said* to me. Those were the first *words* I had *heard* since Grandmother died.

"So you know, he told me about another Listener, a man who was alone as I was, but he lived far away from my village. I had to choose to leave my family, my people, my home. I didn't want to leave them, but I needed my own mate, a Listener like me."

Giggling, Roe crossed her legs and winked at Sarai. "I must confess," she continued. "I really wanted a man. When Z'Shar brought me here and I saw Mar, I felt the heat in me right away and I was on him before we had even spoken aloud, although we were *saying* everything to each other with our inner voices. Mar was very willing. People laughed—they said that was the quickest mating they ever saw."

"They watched you!"

"Oh no," Roe laughed. "Mar got me to his hut. But I suppose they probably heard us… I think we still sometimes wake people at night, especially in this cavern where the alcoves are so close. I think Crue is usually asleep. I'm glad he has a small alcove next to us. But he seems to know what is going on. He is growing so fast! He plays mostly with older children."

"You have been together since then. Have you never wanted another man?"

"No. It is simple and clear. You know these things when you are a Listener."

Sarai nodded. She remembered how she had desired Z'Shar when she first ran into him on the Temple steps.

Just so, said Roe. *We know the day we meet. It feels good and does not pass.* She grinned. "Ariza had to learn this. When he first came to us, he wanted every woman he saw. I *heard* he wanted me, too, but he understood Mar, Crue and I were bonded, so his attentions went to others. Since he couldn't bear the cold when he first got here, he didn't start taking all the women right away. That was hard for him." She stopped, laughing at the memory. "Shanga wanted him. She waited, watching him. They bonded the first day she touched him. He never knew another woman here. That's the way it is for us. It is easy to love each other."

"But if you love each other so much, why do you not have more children?"

"I asked Z'Shar about this," she answered, her face earnest. "He said Listeners usually do not have more than one child. Perhaps it is because the *hearing* bond is so deep."

SIXTEEN

Sarai learned there was another part to the joy the people shared. She *heard* it in their hearts and listened to them speak of it every day. All of the mountain people spoke of the One, a Great Spirit that was not man or woman, giant or earthling. Sarai had often longed for a God she could trust, someone to love and help her. When the rains started, she *heard* her Masters talk scornfully about a man who spoke with one, all-powerful God who had told him to build a great boat, an ark that would ride above the flood of waters. She remembered their words when the people of the mountain community spoke about the Nameless One, although she did not understand this One Spirit that was not a man, an animal or a tree. Perhaps Spirit was the Earth or the skies above—or was It both of these?

One afternoon she sat with Roe and Crue by the wide window. Crue got to his feet and pressed his nose into the smooth, transparent barrier, trying to track individual snowflakes with his quick eyes. Then he pulled his face away and drew pictures with a finger in the film his breath had left. Roe, her dark eyes glowing, tried to answer Sarai's questions about the One Who Is Everywhere. "Yes," she said, "the Great Spirit is the Earth and the skies and One Spirit is All, flowing through all of us, the love we feel for each other. Look at my son, Crue. He hugs us all. He feels all of us in the One."

"I don't—feel Spirit," said Sarai, confused. This idea, this feeling was both new and mysterious to her. "I don't feel anything like what you say."

You will understand, Roe *told* her, wordlessly. *When you are ready, you will find the One has always been with you.*

Sarai sighed. Roe kissed her cheek and said aloud, "Crue, come sit with us. Sarai, listen to Crue. Watch him. He can teach you. He has always known the Way as he calls It."

Crue sat cross-legged in front of Sarai and took her hands with his. He looked straight into her eyes, smiling gently. He was quiet, calm as a warm breeze on a summer evening. He was not afraid of anything.

You don't know any fear, said Sarai in wonder.

No fear. I don't need fear.

Is that how it feels to know Everywhere Spirit?

It is one way I know The Way. There are more ways to know than you can imagine.

You just showed me one way. Thank you.

I am happy to share.

As the gray days faded one into another, Sarai continued to *listen* to Crue and to the others, especially Grandfather. With Grandfather Mendano, she thought she came closest to understanding the Spirit that was in all of them. She loved him deeply and *knew* his great love for her and that awareness moved her more than any words. It was he who taught her most about love and her *hearing* hastened his teachings.

Grandfather could not *hear* her, nor could he *hear* any of the other Listeners. It seemed the *hearing* had not come to him through his alien heritage and he did not sense that Sarai often *heard* him and eagerly tried to *speak* to him, but could never *reach* him. One evening when the gray sky was turning black, Sarai made her way back to the alcove she shared with him. She thought she *heard* him resting and laughing there. Indeed, she found him resting naked, with one of the women not yet mated cuddled next to him, her head on his shoulder. Surprised, Sarai smiled at the lovers and quietly left. After that encounter, when she returned to be with him she *listened* for *signs* that he was coupling, so she did not stumble upon him with a lover again. Grandfather Mendano was a remarkably young old man.

It was at those times when he was full with feeling that she could *hear* the old man and then she loved him the most and thought she felt the Spirit within her. If she lay awake as he slept and dreamt in their alcove, his inner voice captivated her and kept her from falling into her own sleep. She was often awake alone in the dark, for it was when she lay down to sleep that her regrets and desires haunted her and kept her from dreaming alongside the other cavern-dwellers. Z'Shar's words burned in her memory: "You chose to live. You can choose not to hate me… After I get you safe, you will not have to see me again."

What a stubborn, bitter fool she had been! He had brought her to her family and the people with whom she belonged. She was happy, truly happy here and all she had shared with him was hatred. She had hated him for all he was not, when in the secret part of her heart she had always longed to be with him. He had won her trust the first day she ran into him on the Temple steps. He was the first person who *listened* to her and *knew* her for who she truly was. When she remembered standing close to him, she grew yielding inside. He was the only man who had ever stirred her, the only man she wanted. She thought that must be because she was more Listener from the skies than woman of the Earth. She was like him; she was his kind.

Still, she was uneasy with her desires, afraid of her feelings. She had never learned to be anything but a servant to the giants. She dreamed of pleasing Z'Shar, but she feared what she wanted from him.

Again, it was compassionate Roe who understood her best. Like a wise older sister, she took Sarai by the hand and led her to the farthest end of the cavern. Pulling their long black cloaks around them, they paused in the chill that blew in from the relentless snows outside, watching the cold, delicate snowflakes that were strong enough to imprison the mountains. Here where the air was always frosty, the people stored their food in the nooks and crannies in the mountain rock.

Sarai remembered when young Crue had showed her where the food was, the day after she arrived at the cavern. He explained to her that Z'Shar brought much food to them—strange, exotic tastes from far away. Then Sarai understood why there were many oranges, melons, dates, pomegranates, berries and vegetables and nuts of all kinds that she had been accustomed to eating in the Gods' Temple. Not so long ago, Z'Shar told them the storms covered this and many other lands, even though this was not the season for heavy snows and rains. In several trips, each time filling up his sky chariot like a huge, flying sack, he had brought them extra food, for the people had not had enough time to gather and store adequate supplies.

Sarai and Roe walked back into the cavern. A good distance beyond the storage area was a sharp turn in the passageway, and around the bend the cavern ceiling sloped down as the walls came closer together. The first fireplace niche was inside the turn and nearby was an empty sleeping alcove, filled with warm furs and two of Z'Shar's long black cloaks resting on top.

Pointing to the alcove, Roe said, "This is where Z'Shar sleeps when he comes to stay with us."

"Oh," was all Sarai could say. She felt the thud of her heart and her knees trembled.

Roe smiled. "I'll leave you here. You'll understand."

"Oh," repeated Sarai.

"It's okay," soothed Roe. "Go, sit in the alcove. Be with him."

"But—he's not there."

"Not in flesh. But that doesn't matter. You will find him for yourself without him being there. The All One will teach you."

Sarai didn't understand how the One who is everywhere was going to come to her and teach her in Z'Shar's alcove. But somehow the space beckoned to her; she wanted to go inside. Roe smiled again and turned away to walk back through the passage. Sarai walked slowly to Z'Shar's alcove, pushed back the furs draped partially in front of it and eased herself down on the cloaks and soft furs piled on the ground.

There seemed to be something like a sleeping pallet beneath the furs; the effect was spongy and comfortable, as though the ground was not rock like the rest of the mountain. She leaned down to rub her face into the smooth cloak on top, trying to breathe in the smell she remembered of him. As always, the black cloak was odorless. So odd; she could not get used to that.

She sat up, knitting her brows in thought and then breathed deeply, calling the Everywhere Spirit to fill her. But she did not feel the Spirit come and she sighed, sad again. She was alone, a little chilly, in Z'Shar's uninhabited alcove.

She stroked the furs with one hand. A tear brimmed and rolled slowly down her cheek. She wanted desperately to beg his forgiveness for her ungrateful ways; she wished she could offer herself to him, please him more than she had ever pleased any of the other giant men. But he had gone searching for more survivors of the storm and his endeavors to help were far more important than her desire to be with him. She was but one stubborn woman among many who were far wiser and certainly more deserving of his love and kindness.

His love. Yes, she knew that was what she wanted from him. And what she feared he would not give her. As much as she had loved Melina in the Gods' Temple and as much as she had grown to love dear Grandfather and the other Listeners who taught her and cared for her in her new cavern home, she loved Z'Shar more. That is why she missed him all night, why she ached when she remembered how she had pushed him away, no matter how much kindness and understanding he had shown her. She wished fervently for his return and knew she would wait as long as she had to.

Resigned, she drew a deep breath, rose from the furs and left the alcove. She found the other Listeners gathered at the cavern center to help prepare the evening meal. She stood by Roe's side, taking her hand. She said, "The Great Spirit did not come to me. But now I understand, just as you said I would. All of you must have known what I could not see for myself. I love Z'Shar."

Roe nodded, smiling. "Now you can tell him, when he returns. And Sarai, don't be so sure the One is not with you. Often we do not recognize the Spirit that is everywhere, perhaps because It is always with us. We are so small and All is vast."

"Teach me more," said Sarai. "I want to know All as you do."

"I can tell you what I feel," Roe said. "Each one of us can tell you what each one feels. But you already live with the One. You only need to recognize how you feel."

Ariza stood nearby, his arm about Shanga's shoulders as they listened quietly. Reaching for Sarai with his other hand, he gently touched her arm and she turned to face him.

"Maybe you understand All One as I do," he said, looking directly into her eyes. "I live in great love from the All One. In One, I love myself. When I love others, All flows from me through to the other and we are One in the Great Spirit."

Indeed, Sarai *felt* his love pass into her. But for her, it was Ariza's love only. She let go of Roe's hand to embrace Ariza and then kiss Shanga. "I feel that I lack something," she said, slowly shaking her head. "I lack the Spirit. I don't *know.* I don't know how."

SEVENTEEN

GENESIS, VII

12 And the rain fell upon the earth forty days and forty nights.

*24 And the waters prevailed upon the earth one hundred and
fifty days.*

The gray and white snows outside surrounded the mountain
cavern for many days and nights. One older man, Coro,
died in his sleep. He was not nearly as old as Grandfather Mendano, but the harsh cold taxed the strength of the people whom
the false Gods had once plucked from warmer lands. This was
not their true home. The God-made cavern protected them from
the bitter cold, but it did not nurture them like the sun's rays and
the earth below their feet. Most people lived short lives.

All of the people mourned the newly dead. They wrapped
themselves in furs and black cloaks for protection from the cold,
biting wind and brought his body to the farthest, longer entrance

to the cavern, where Sarai had first come with Z'Shar. Just inside the entrance was a fire pit. Mar and Ariza made a fire and used its heat to melt the snows outside the entrance. With heavy sticks, Coro's three sons and his brother dug a grave in the wet ground, laid the man to rest and hastily covered him up with icy wet earth. Soon the snow would hide his grave forever. Each snow season, too many beloved were buried, forever hidden just outside the cavern haven.

Later, a child was born dead. All the people grieved with the young parents, their faces wet with tears. This was their first child. Many babies died early in the cold world high in the mountains. Had the smothering snows not come during this usually warmer season, the small one might have seen the sunlight and lived.

Worrying that her child would also be born during the long storm, Shanga was counting each day that the snows fell. She took a stick and etched a line where the cavern floor was soft next to her alcove for each day that kept her and Ariza within the great cavern. When she had counted thirty days and thirty nights, the quiet snows melted into thick sheets of rain that pummeled the giant window and slowly melted the mounded snows.

Sarai stared outside below the cavern, watching the huge Temple and mighty trees emerge from under the disappearing white blanket. The ancient trees and stone buildings stood in the waters, half-way drowned. She was grateful for the artificial shelter that had given her and the rest of the people a warm home during the storms.

She thought about the giants who had used the mountain people and so easily abandoned them. The men from the skies had done many wondrous things with their weapons, created this cavern and other places that were strange and hard to understand. Even after the Gods departed, their mark remained upon earthly places. Here in the high valley, the people of Earth whom the Gods had left behind huddled in the spacious cavern to survive the conquering winter, as they had for more generations than they could remember. The people were not prepared for the snows that had come in summer, but Z'Shar had helped them. The little group would live through the floods that covered the Earth.

Unlike the whispers of the falling snows, the drumming of the rains was familiar to Sarai from the land of her birth. At times the thunder still roared at the mountain and the rains poured down to the Earth. But more often the rains were gentle and light, as though they wanted to warm and cleanse the frozen land. At those times, Sarai bundled herself in furs and visited one or another of the cavern entrances so she could watch and listen to the soothing water from the skies. When the storm pounded above the cavern, she smiled, reminded that she was safe in her new home.

EIGHTEEN

Several nights after the snows turned to rain, Sarai lay awake and wide-eyed in the dark alcove. Grandfather Mendano cried out in his sleep, thrusting his long legs out from under the fur he had wrapped himself in. She *heard* his dream*: His breath ragged, he ran after his daughter Zillah, calling her to come to safety in the high mountain cavern. Zillah did not hear him, for she fled in terror from the advancing sea waters, her long black hair streaming behind her in the wind. She called for her children and he called to her and the children, but no one heard him.*

Had Sarai not already been awake, his dream would have roused her. How he longed for his beloved family! But they, too, had perished when the rain and seas flooded the land. She *reached* for him, tried to soothe his fears and wake him from the terror of his dream. But as always, he could not *hear* her. She rolled close to him, felt for his jerking legs with her hands and covered them with the black cloak that Z'Shar had given her. He moaned and then lay still; the dream vanished from both of them. Sarai sighed, glad that he was back in untroubled sleep. His age made the cold much harder to bear and he tired easily. He needed so much rest. She lay down next to him and closed her eyes.

She sat up and blinked. She realized she could see the outline of his form under the cloak and fur. The gray day must have emerged from the black night. Had she slept? Yawning, she lay down again, pulling a large fur over her. She felt as tired as though she had just settled down for the night. She breathed deeply and let herself sink into desired sleep.

She dreamt she *heard* Z'Shar, *calling* to her from within the cavern, "Sarai, will you come to me? Will you talk with me?"

Heart pounding, she woke. She sat up in the dim light, hearing voices near the alcove. She rubbed her eyes, trying to make out the words, but the speakers had moved farther away. She put her hands over her heart, as though she could quiet it with her touch. Her dream felt very close, as though Z'Shar was in the cavern, *reaching* for her with his *voice*.

He was. She *heard* him as she sat near Grandfather. Again he *called* to her, *Sarai, come, be with me. Let me talk with you.*

A big warm bubble burst in her chest and made ripples down to her feet. *I am coming,* she *answered.*

Her heart still pounded in her ears. She reached for her tunic near the alcove wall and pulled it over her head. Then she found the black trousers, thrust her legs into them and pulled them up over her hips. She did not want to take the cloak from Grandfather's legs, nor did she want to wake him. She pushed herself to the opening of the alcove and slid down to the cavern floor, where she found her black boots waiting.

She stood for a moment, looking around the central eating area. She was glad Grandfather had selected this alcove, where the cavern was warmest. There were fruits and nuts still scattered around the long table, leftovers from the evening meal. She gathered them in her hands and ate quickly. Spotting a jug of water at the far end of the table, she washed down her hasty meal and slaked her thirst. Then she walked quickly towards the washing area at the far end of the cavern. People scurried past her, talking excitedly to each other, telling the good news.

"Z'Shar has come back!"

"Z'Shar! It has been long. Perhaps he could no longer fly his boat in the storm. Where is he? Did he have something to eat?"

"Yes, early, when he returned. He is resting now, in his place. He says he will stay for many days this time."

"Good! I am happy. Perhaps he waits for his mother. She has not come for many moons."

"Yes, I hope she comes soon. I love to see Mother."

Sarai paused, listening to what their words told her. Z'Shar had a mother; she had come here before. It was as she had believed—the giants were only big men, so there had to be giant women who bore their children. She could have been one of the mothers herself...

She hurried to the wash area. With intimate care, she washed and made herself ready for Z'Shar, hoping he would desire her to pleasure him. Surely he would want her! She knew he had wanted her before, the first day they had touched and *spoken* on the Temple steps. She meant to give herself to him wholly. She would pleasure him in any way he wanted. It would be enough for her that he touched her and held her close to him, took her for himself. Returning to the cavern center, she *called* to Z'Shar again, *I come to you now.*

I am glad, Sarai. If it pleases you, come to my alcove.

Grateful tears welled up in her eyes. She had waited many days to ask his forgiveness. Her yearning for him was strong. *Yes, it pleases me,* she *said.*

She sprinted to his alcove and halted, breathless, several arms-lengths from it. Z'Shar stood at its open entrance wearing his habitual black clothing except for his cloak, which she saw on top of the furs within the alcove. His face was impassive. She *heard* nothing, *felt* nothing from him. She ached. She had grown accustomed to *feeling* everything from the other Listeners and had forgotten that she could not *hear* him unless he allowed it. Stinging tears brimmed over her eyelids and fell silently from her chin to the ground.

"I did not know if you would see me," he said, his eyes fixed on hers. "I promised that you would not have to see me again. But you have come. Perhaps—perhaps you no longer hate me."

"No!" she cried. "No, I don't hate you. You already *know* how I feel. I was so angry and foolish. I come to beg your forgiveness. I know how wrong I was. I *am* like you! I am more your kind than I am like a person of Earth. I have learned so much. I wish—I wish to give myself to you. Please forgive me!"

Still she *heard* only emptiness from him, although her nipples grew taut at the sight of him and she felt a pulse between her thighs. He stared into her eyes. "Sarai," he said her name with a sigh, "I was never angry with you. I don't need to forgive you anything. I am happy you have come. I thought of you all the time I was away."

"Then you will have me, all of me!" she exclaimed and fell at his feet. "I only want to love you. You know I want you. You knew it on the Temple steps."

As he had back then, Z'Shar knelt and pulled her up in front of him. "I know," he whispered and stroked her black hair around her face. *I love you, Sarai.*

With a gasp, Sarai *felt* him embrace her naked body, though he only touched her hair and her hand. But as her woman parts made ready to receive him, the feeling vanished, as though he was not ready to share it with her. He said, "You should be able to keep your secret feelings from me if you choose. I want to teach you now, if you will let me."

She could never predict what this man would do, what he wanted. He was always different than the others. She looked into his eyes and said, "If that is what you wish. I only want to please you. I know you have much to teach me."

He smiled and nodded. "Good. Then step back a little, so we do not touch."

She did as he instructed.

"You only need to draw in your breath, hold and choose what you wish to hide."

"But I don't choose to hide anything from you!" she protested. "I want you to know all of my feelings."

"I understand, Sarai. But it is important to me. I do not want to have this power over you, knowing you whether you wish it or not. We are the same kind. I am not your God. This is what I want: I want you to be able to block me from you, if so you choose."

Sarai stared at him and swallowed. "If that is what you wish then I will learn. Tell me again."

Z'Shar drew a breath and smiled. "Thank you. Now, breathe in and choose to block your desires from me. It is simple, but you may have to try a few times."

With three breaths, three tries, she *knew* she had succeeded. He *listened* and *probed* for her yearning, but he could not *touch* her or *hear* her desire. She ached inside, but was glad that she had done as he asked.

"Yes," he mused out loud. "You are more of us than of Earth. You can learn all that I know."

"But I feel myself—more of Earth," she said.

"You will always feel the Earth in you, no matter how much you learn of the rest of you. Earth is strong in you. I love that part of you, how different you are."

"I don't want to block you! I don't want this power!" she burst out.

"Yes," he said. "How well I know it. Now you understand how I felt with you, why I needed to teach you to shut me out. Wait just a little longer, Sarai. I want you to *hear* all of me."

An invisible gate opened and a vast loneliness rushed like a wave from within him, crashing upon her. She stumbled backwards, falling. He jumped forward and caught her, pulling her next to him. Her ear rested over his heart and she heard its steady thumping. Z'Shar shook, crying.

You thought you were all alone when the floods came, he *said, but you were not. There were others right here. But I am the only Listener from my world here on the Earth. I was banished to live out the rest of my days on Earth when others from my Home World discovered I was helping the people of Earth resist them whenever I could. 'You love these Earth people so much,' they sneered, 'you can live with them until you die.'*

We don't know how, but my father found out that my mother and I were Listeners. Even after all the time they were bonded, he hated her and ordered her to leave his dwelling, her home, forbade her to be near him. She fled to the place where the Listeners must stay, away from the others on Home World. You have heard how they hate us. Father told those in command of the Earth journeys and they found me here.

My mother risks expulsion to visit me here when it is warm enough. The Listeners have one ship—one sky chariot—that brings them here and they love to visit the people of Earth. The others, those who are not Listeners, no longer come here to the high mountains, so it is safe for my mother to come here. But we don't know how long the others will allow us to travel outside our Home World.

I have lived alone on Earth for almost ten years. They found out I helped Mendano escape from them, although they don't know I brought him here to the safe place. They have forgotten about this cavern. I rest here, among the people I know and love, but I long for other Listeners, so I spend time searching for them.

123

When I saw you, Sarai, when I heard you, I knew you were more like me than anyone else I had encountered in this world. You made me happy and I laughed for the first time in many years. I reached you, I touched your heart. I thought with you I would no longer feel alone. But you hated me because I was one of the giants. You didn't know then that we were the same kind and you refused to believe me when I told you. I wanted so much just to be with you, to love you and share everything with you. I didn't know how to make you believe that I loved you, all that you are. I brought you here so that you would understand who you are and that you are not alone. I did not know until I listened to you this morning that Mendano is your grandfather. But I knew you were like me.

He hugged her tighter. *I couldn't bear for you to think you must serve me, like you served the other men in the Temple. So I taught you to block your love, just for a little while, so you would feel I am the man who loves you, the man you love—not your Master. I wanted you to choose to love me.*

I loved you before I knew I was choosing it, said Sarai. *I want no power over you. Here, I release all of it, I give you all my secrets!* She expelled her breath and let go the blocks, fresh tears flowing down her face.

Joy washed through them from one to the other. Laughing, Z'Shar pulled her into the alcove, letting the long furs fall down over the opening. He pushed her down on the mound of furs and cloaks and stooped to pull off each of her long, black boots. He lay down beside her. *Now, now we can love each other.* Taking her chin in his hand, he lifted her face to his mouth and kissed her forehead, each green eye, the tip of her nose and hungrily, her mouth.

Sarai trembled in her wanting, but she was eager to please him. "I will do anything to pleasure you," she promised. "Just tell me what you like."

Z'Shar stroked her slowly, gently, from her head to her legs. "There is little you need to do. We will pleasure each other," he said. He pulled his shirt over his head and then tugged at Sarai's black coverings.

"I don't understand—" she began as she wriggled out of her tunic.

"Before now you have only pleasured your Masters. Today we bond as we love each other."

She *heard* his desires and reached for him while he touched her the way he *knew* she wanted. When she touched him, moved against him, he *shared* all that he felt. He kissed and caressed her in ways she had never known, arousing deeper desires. For the first time, she opened fully to her lover. They forgot everything but their joy and pleasure together.

NINETEEN

Much later, they lay spent beside each other. Sarai rested her head on his shoulder and dozed. She dreamt she was back in the land of her birth, swimming in the warm, friendly sea. She felt as one with the sea-water of the Earth. She woke, opened her eyes and caressed his naked chest. Z'Shar planted a kiss in her hair and she drew her leg over him, savoring the warmth of his flesh against hers.

"You didn't sleep long. Do you need more of me?" he teased.

"Not yet." She smiled. "I had a dream."

"Yes, I *heard*. You were happy in the sea."

"Yes and it was something more. It was like being with you, like I was joined with the water. And I wonder... Z'Shar, I have been trying to understand the One, the Spirit Who Is Everywhere. Mar and Roe and the people who live here, they know the One, but I do not. But now I feel different..." She sat up and stretched.

Z'Shar also sat up, quiet as his dark eyes traveled over her. He reached for her chin and tilted her face to look into her eyes. "You have changed today. You have found more of yourself."

"Oh, yes! I never thought… Z'Shar, do you *know* the One?"

"Yes."

"Then why can't I find It? They say the One is with me, in all ways—or that I already live the Way—but I don't feel anything…"

"We all live the Way, Sarai."

"Everyone says that."

He grinned. "Yes, they do. But now that we are bonded, I can *hear* more of you. I *hear* you opening, reaching to understand. I think that until you came here you lived only a small part of yourself, the Sarai who is born of the Earth. And the Earth woman is young and strong, like this Earth." He let go of her chin, put his arms around her and pulled her down with him.

Sarai cuddled next to him, her head on his shoulder again. "I only know the Earth."

"Yes, love. And I know that more of you is of my Home World and still a mystery to you. You are blessed, for you are also a Listener and so few of us are. Not knowing, you lived hating your own kind. That part of you was always hidden from the woman of Earth."

She sighed. "Now I must also be Sarai of the Home World, only that is not my home. I don't know how to do this."

"I am no God." Z'Shar laughed out loud. "But I see so much of you. Live as your whole self, sweet Sarai. Enjoy all of you. Certainly you have felt whole with me, yes?" He kissed her mouth. "Feel deeply, find your whole self and don't lose any more of your life hating. I think then the sun will burst through the clouds and you will feel as All One."

TWENTY

Perhaps if Z'Shar and Sarai had truly been Gods, their joyous lovemaking might have sustained them for many days. But they were a mortal man and a mortal woman and they were hungry when the day grew to a close. Laughing, they helped each other dress in their black clothing. Stepping outside the stone alcove, Z'Shar knelt to hold Sarai's tall boots while she thrust each bare foot inside, down to the bottom. She stood up beside him and he drew her into a long embrace, kissing her until she giggled and pushed him away. "I have to breathe!"

"There will be time for that," he said, hugging her again. "Right now, I'm not sure I'm ready to share you with anyone else." He sighed. "Ah, but I'm hungry."

"Me too."

He released her and took her hand. They walked towards the cavern center. "Try to stay close to me as we share the evening meal. I will have many people to greet." He continued wordlessly, *Even if we get separated, we can talk with our inner voices all the while we are among others. I will be happy to see them.*

As though expecting them, Crue sprang up and rushed to hug Sarai and Z'Shar before they reached the long, low wooden table where people sat on furs laid over the ground, enjoying food and company. Getting in between them with an arm reaching around each of their waists, Crue led them over to sit behind Mar and Roe. Before they could grasp some food or say a word, many excited people crowded around to welcome Z'Shar.

"Z'Shar!" Daza, a small, bright-eyed girl, ran to Z'Shar, sat in his lap and raised her head, looking backwards to smile into his down-turned face. "I'm so happy you are here! I love you, Z'Shar."

"Z'Shar, I missed you when you came home," said Keiko, her mother. "It was so early. I was sleeping."

"Will you stay longer this time?" asked three people at once. "It's still raining," said one. "But the snows have stopped," interrupted another.

Many more clamored for his attention. Reaching his long arm to the table, Z'Shar grabbed a handful of fruits, nuts, seeds, dried fish, whatever his nimble fingers encountered. He fed himself with one hand and hugged his welcomers with his free arm. Daza smiled contentedly in his lap.

Crue sat next to Sarai, hugging her. With a start, she *heard* him and blushed. *Oh my! He knows. He is basking in our happiness from our lovemaking!*

Ever sensitive, Crue also *heard* how hungry she was. Crawling over her and between his parents, he grabbed three dates off the table and popped one into her waiting mouth. Then much to little Daza's annoyance, he squeezed next to Z'Shar and stretched his arms around the big man's hips, laying his ear next to the man's stomach. He giggled, listening to the rumblings inside. Daza stuck out her bottom lip and grasped Z'Shar's smooth black trousers with both chubby little hands, so that Crue's head would not dislodge her from her coveted position.

Watching him with Crue, Sarai was surprised to see Z'Shar flush under his dark skin. Then with a shout, he burst out laughing. Tears fell down his cheeks and his entire body shook, delighting Daza who still clutched his trousers.

I forgot we were among other Listeners, he *said* to Sarai, shrugging his shoulders. *There are some things I do not want to share with everyone. I forgot to put up my own blocks! That has never happened before.* His laughter slowed to chuckling. *I was so happy to be with you that I did not think of anything else. But I will remember to make my blocks from now on.*

Too late. Roe winked at him. *We all know.*

Chewing pumpkin seeds and carrots, Sarai *asked, Could you hear us—everything?—while we loved each other?*

Not everything. Roe smiled. She said aloud, "But I am afraid Crue is more sensitive than the rest of us, so I can't be sure what he *hears.*" She turned to Z'Shar and teased, "I do recognize your hunger, my friend."

Again, Z'Shar's face reddened. He swallowed. Then he broke into more peals of laughter. When he paused to draw breath, Mar spoke up. "It is good to see you laughing, Z'Shar," he said earnestly. "I hurt when you were sad."

Tiring of competing for space with Crue's head, Daza crawled out of Z'Shar's lap and wandered off in search of her mother.

Z'Shar reached his arm for Sarai, drawing her close to him. *No more sadness,* he *told* Mar. *Now I, too, have a mate.*

Then Grandfather lowered himself to the ground beside Sarai. She cried out and hugged the smiling, white-haired man. Mendano did not need to *hear* her to see the change that had come over her. He knew her very well. It was not the first time he had seen someone in his family full in the glow of love.

"I am so glad you're here," she said. "I guess you know where I was."

"Everyone knows now." He smiled in return. "I heard Z'Shar was back as soon as I woke up. I believe I have some words for him, too. It is my duty as your Grandfather."

Z'Shar was again besieged by the people who loved him. Crue had finally let go of his belly and moved next to the table where he could reach more food. Clasping Sarai's hand, Grandfather Mendano waited patiently behind the greeters who thronged around Z'Shar. Eventually, they moved next to him and rested on the furs that blanketed the ground until no one remained between them.

"Z'Shar, please stand." Grandfather spoke solemnly in his native tongue, attempting to sound formal. The three of them rose to their feet. Fixing his blue eyes on the other man's face, Grandfather Mendano continued, "Z'Shar, you have brought my granddaughter to me and now you will take her away."

"I would not take her away from you!" Z'Shar protested in Mendano's language, a smile playing at his lips.

"Well, it would appear she will no longer stay with me while I sleep," countered the old man. He bit his lip to keep from laughing. "Who will clean up after me now? She is the only one who does that."

"Oh, I will still clean the alcove," said Sarai.

"Not necessary," Grandfather waved her off. "But you, Z'Shar," he went on, knitting his eyebrows, "you will take good care of my granddaughter, provide well for her like any man who married my kin in the land where I was born. Make her happy or you will answer to me."

"Yes, I will. I promise." Z'Shar bowed his head to the old man. Then he abruptly threw his arms about him and the two friends embraced heartily.

"It is good to see you, Z'Shar," said Mendano, when the two men released each other. "I wish you had not stayed away so long."

Z'Shar shook his head. "I needed to keep looking," he said thoughtfully and pointed to the huge window in the cavern wall. "Look out to the flooded valley below us. Below these mountains the rains have flooded the Earth. The seas swelled and washed over the land. Nothing was left uncovered—no people, no cities, no life. Not even the birds that flew above us lived through the rain."

Mendano hung his bearded head, a tear escaping his eye. "I feared as much. I dreamt many times of—my daughter. Even last night, I dreamt she would perish. I could not save her! Sometimes I wish you had not saved me from the other giants, Z'Shar. I was prepared to die, although then I would never have known Sarai... But I miss Zillah so."

Sarai remembered Grandfather's dream from the early morning. She clasped his hand and squeezed gently. "Then there is no one left alive but us here?" she asked Z'Shar, wishing the great floods were only a dream.

Z'Shar brightened. "Come, let's sit down again." As they sat, he assured her, "There are those who escaped the floods—people and animals, birds, creatures of the sea and more. But most of them are far, far away from here." He turned to Roe and took her hands in his. "I have been to your village," he told her. "They are safe. They were above the floods and they took refuge in the caves, just as they do in the winter. But some of them, the older ones especially, got sick and died."

"My mother, my brothers, my father—"

"Yes, all of them, they are well, along with many others. I brought them extra food."

"Oh, thank you! Z'Shar, I want to go there, I want to see them."

He nodded. "I will take you there, as soon as the rains stop and it is warm enough. You have been too long without seeing your family."

Letting go of her hands, he turned and spoke to the group. "Here, in the lands where most of you were born, there is also one family: a man called Noah and his wives and children, and their mates and children—"

"I have heard of him!" Sarai interrupted excitedly. "I *heard* the Gods—the giants talking about this man when I was still in the Temple. They were laughing at him because they thought he was mad. They said he claimed the One God told him to build a big boat, an ark, and gather his family and many animals from the Earth… Oh, I don't remember everything, but they lived, didn't they?"

Z'Shar nodded. "I have seen the ark and visited the people, though I was there less than a day. It was not my place to be there. The ark is large, but small when it is the only dry place for many beings. There is no way they could come to this place either, even if there weren't so many of them. We are too far away."

"Did the Great Spirit really talk to him?" asked Shanga. She and Ariza had joined the other Listeners while Z'Shar spoke to the group.

"Yes," replied Z'Shar, "he told me God had instructed him what to do. He believes the One God spoke to him with words."

"I have not heard anyone here speak of the One as God, or that the Spirit spoke as a man does," said Ariza, his brows knitted in thought. Then he smiled. "But I have heard many strange things. If I had never come, I would not have believed this place was here. I am glad to see you, Z'Shar. I think you waited too long to come back to Sarai."

Everybody knows, mused Sarai.

Everyone in this mountain, said Roe.

I told you, Z'Shar said to Sarai. *There are times when you will want to block your secrets from other people.*

"Not fair," protested Grandfather, watching their smiles. "Speak the words we can all hear!"

TWENTY-ONE

On the seventh day after Z'Shar came home to the Mountain People, the rains did not fall. The people gathered by the window the Gods had made, staring outside at the still, cloudy skies and the murky waters below. Sarai watched the massive trees standing strong in the flood, taller than the Gods' Temples lurking in the watery depths. The life of Earth outlasted and overcame the invasions of the giant vermin from the skies. But how much nectar had they sucked from her flowers, how much wealth had the false gods stripped from the Earth? Would the Great Flood keep them from returning? How long could the cavern-dwellers' little community last if the waters continued to cover the Earth?

Shanga touched her arm, startling Sarai out of her reverie. And then she opened her mouth in a soft cry, for she *felt* wonderful happiness in the woman big with child.

Shanga smiled, glowing. "I wanted to tell you," she said breathily. "I awoke in the night and I could *hear* my child! I have never felt anything like this. I have never felt so happy!"

Overcome, Sarai hugged the shorter woman to her breast and kissed the top of her head.

"I only *hear* the child," Shanga continued, her voice a little muffled against Sarai, "but I know that is because she lives in me. She is a girl, a big strong girl. She *speaks* to me—not with words, but I *feel* her... It is so new to me. This morning Ariza *heard* her too."

Sarai was so happy for her that she started to cry. Shanga's smooth brown arms reached around her friend. "I know you will *hear* your child, too," she said. "Roe told us she *heard* Crue very early when he came to live within her."

Sarai stepped back. "Am I with child?"

Shanga laughed. "You are so funny, Sarai. Sometimes you are like a child yourself. You and Z'Shar are mated. Everybody knows it. Your Grandfather knows it well. It will not be long. You will be a mother and you will *hear* your child. You will know this joy." She rubbed her swollen belly with great tenderness. "Oh yes," she added. "You will know all of this and you will be hungry all the time, too. Want to get something to eat with me?"

Sarai shook her head. "No, not now. I want to be alone with my thoughts. I need to think about this, about having a child with Z'Shar. I am very happy for you, Shanga. Please tell me more later about what you are *hearing.*" Shanga nodded and ambled off to the eating area.

Alone, Sarai blushed happily. She felt the truth of Shanga's words. Since priestesses of the Temple had rarely born children of their Masters, Sarai had not thought about bearing a child of Z'Shar's. But when she lived with the other priestesses in the

Temple, she had thought she was of the Earth, just like the other women. She reminded herself she should live her whole being now, to be a woman of both the Earth and of the skies above. Her hopes blossomed like roses in her heart. To bear a child with the man she loved! She would know the joys that Shanga had shared and she would love her child as Grandfather Mendano had loved his Zillah, her mother, whom she had never known.

A distant memory stirred then, singing softly like a bird returning home. As in her dream of being one with the sea waters as she lay in Z'Shar's arms, she felt very small, warm, floating in salt water in a safe, dark cove, protected from the cold rains outside. Like the gentle waters that suspended her, held her, the sonorous voice was all around her, warm inside her, always with her. She was remembering her mother.

She *called* to Z'Shar, *I have something to tell you. I remember!*

Soon, he *answered.*

She knew he would be surrounded by the mountain folk. She rarely had her new mate to herself, for he was always accompanied by the people who loved him. They talked excitedly with him, full of love for the giant man from the skies. They were not Listeners, so the sharing took much longer. And always, they asked him when his mother would return; they loved her as much as they loved him. Z'Shar sighed and told them, "I miss her, too. But she cannot come while the skies are storming. We must wait for the sun to return and dry up the waters."

Today at last the rains had stopped and the people were happy, talking all day to Z'Shar about how his mother would soon be with them. Watching him with the people, Sarai smiled and hugged herself. Z'Shar loved the people of the Earth; he was fascinated, delighted with them. As he had told Sarai, he also told the other mountain-dwellers, "You are a young people, vibrant with new life, fertile with many children. You live with many hardships. When the rains end you will be strong; you will thrive on the Earth and bear many more children. There must be many of you, for few survive the challenges of the Earth to live a long life. I come from a world of an old, old people. We have few children, but they all grow very old, just like our Home World."

Opening himself wide he listened intently, learned from them, probed their different ways as though tasting them on his tongue. Sarai *heard* the man she loved learning new ideas, experimenting in his mind with thoughts that only people of the Earth knew and striving to feel as a man of the Earth might. Since Sarai was part woman of the Earth, she had lived with those feelings all her life and never questioned them. But Z'Shar was always learning: the Earth had been his home for only ten years.

She would share her memory of her mother with Z'Shar later, perhaps when they lay down to sleep in their alcove. She smiled again and drew a breath. Maybe after their lovemaking.

Now she wanted to find Grandfather Mendano and tell him she remembered her mother, his beloved Zillah. Her long strides took her quickly towards his alcove. He was standing in front of it, wrapping himself with a long, thick fur over his black clothing as he always did. Still, he shivered. But he smiled when Sarai reached him and hugged her with one arm. "Ah, will I ever feel warm again?"

She laughed. "Of course you will. We all will. Come and look out the great window. Or we can go to the cavern entrance. You can see the rains have stopped."

"Ah, yes! That is what I have waited to hear. To the window then."

They hurried back to the window and stood next to it, seeing their breath form on the clear barrier to the outside. Silent together, they gazed out at the cold, gray day. Save for the giant trees bending in the wind, they saw nothing else living. Only dark, murky waters.

"Grandfather Mendano." Sarai broke the silence and looked at him. "I want to tell you something."

He turned his face to hers. "Tell me, child."

"I have remembered my mother, Zillah."

He took her hand. "You remember her? How is this? She gave you up when you were born."

Sarai sighed. "I only remember her from when I was still within her."

"You remember her then? That is a miracle! What did she look like?"

"I don't know. I was—inside her. I only *heard* her. I felt her."

He frowned, cocked his head. "Tell me. What did you feel?"

"Warm, like I was in a warm sea. Like she held me inside her. I was happy. Often I was tired. I slept."

Grandfather gently dropped her hand and, sighing, looked down at the ground. "Ah, I wish I could *hear* like you. I wish I could see what you see."

Sarai thought of the times when she could easily *hear* him: when he was full of feeling; when he lay with a woman; when he dreamt of Zillah. Then, there by the great window, she *heard* him and *saw* him hug his black-haired daughter to him, kissing her forehead. Instinctively, she *reached* into their embrace, joining her love with his, so that it seemed she held Zillah next to her, felt the beating of her mother's heart.

Grandfather caught his breath and raised his head. His blue eyes widened, staring into her eyes. Tears rolled down his cheeks, though he did not make a sound. He trembled. Sarai caught his arm to steady him.

He let go of his breath and closed his eyes. "It's gone," he murmured, "but I *heard* you. You saw her through my eyes. You felt what I felt. We were like one person."

"Is that what they mean?" Sarai wondered aloud. "We are all One."

Mendano opened his eyes and waved his hand, as if dismissing everyone else and whatever they knew. "I don't know." He shook his head. "I don't care right now. Here is what I do know. You love me and you love Zillah. And you shared her with me. I love you, Sarai."

He pulled her into a hug, the way he used to hug her mother. She felt his tears wet her neck and remembered what Ariza had said: "The All One is within me. When my love flows to you, we are One in the All."

She began to understand.

TWENTY-TWO

The rains did not return. But oppressive gray clouds still barred the sun from the mountain folk and each day the restless people stared down at the dark waters that possessed their valley homeland. Though they considered themselves fortunate to have a haven from the bitter cold, they mourned the loss of warmer days and being outside. They longed to walk free among the tall trees under changing skies while they searched for sweet and tart berries in the valley. They wanted to breathe the fresh, rain-washed air and drink pure water from the rivers and streams that criss-crossed the fertile land. They feared if the sun did not break through the clouds, the waters would not recede. They also worried where they would find animals to hunt for meat, since the storms had drowned the entire valley. They could use the giants' Temple for shelter, but where would they find enough food?

Knowing their beloved Z'Shar would help them through hardship, the people did not despair, but waited impatiently for the sun to warm the land and free them from their enclosed life in the cavern. Shanga and Ariza were determined to welcome their child into the open air. Each day they watched for the sun to appear. Mar, Roe and Crue told all the cavern-dwellers about each place in the valley they would visit when the sun returned and the waters dried up. Grandfather promised to run across the valley on his bare feet, even while the ground was still muddy.

The wait was easier for Sarai, for the vast cavern was the first place she had ever felt at home. As she learned from the love of Z'Shar, Grandfather and the others, she felt her inner being flourish like a forest teeming with life. Z'Shar encouraged her to take time each day to look inward and concentrate on the place where her *hearing* came through. This was also, he said, the place where the Great Spirit came through her, where she could feel the One who was always with her.

With daily practice her *hearing* grew stronger, so Z'Shar continued her education. He began teaching her to use her wind. When the two laughing giants appeared suddenly at various places in the cavern, the children would squeal with delight. Everyone cheered and congratulated Sarai on her progress.

Many days after the rains stopped, the morning light woke her. Beside her Z'Shar sat cross-legged, naked under his cloak. She *heard* him *listening* to someone far away.

She's coming, he *told* her, so happy the sun seemed to shine through him. *I can hear her now. My mother is close to the Earth. And there are many other Listeners with her. Usually she does not come with so many, in such a big sky ship. Something has changed.*

When will they be here?

142

"Soon," he said aloud. "Come, it is late and very light. We can join the others for the morning meal."

"Very light," she agreed, wriggling out from beneath one of the black cloaks. Wondering why they had slept so long into the morning, she thrust her arms and legs into black coverings and pulled the hood of her cloak over her head. Crawling over the furs strewn across the alcove floor, she spied her black boots and pushed her feet into them, glad for the protection from the cold ground. Dressed in the same way, Z'Shar pushed aside the furs over the doorway and followed her out into the passage.

Outside their covered alcove, bright light streamed into the cavern at the nearby bend in the rock walls. Startled by the sound of many voices, they turned to see several people running towards the light, like moths drawn to a flame. Z'Shar and Sarai looked excitedly at each other, grasped hands and joined the group of runners. As one, the people burst through to the wide cavern entrance and into the glorious bright sunlight. They raised their hands high, as though they could pull it closer to themselves and to the Earth.

Then, like a flame snuffed out, the sun was smothered by dark clouds. Sarai shivered and snuggled closer to Z'Shar. *Did I really see the sun?* she wondered. *Will it ever return? Should I run and wake Grandfather so that he can see the sun or would he be disappointed if it did not come again?* She saw others holding hands, staring at the clouds as though they had never seen the sky before. Someone cried. Another wailed, "Sun! Come back!"

And the sun answered. Like a powerful God pushing his way

through thick vines and undergrowth the sun burst through, shoving the dark clouds to either side and revealing deep blue skies. The people jumped and shouted with joy, welcoming the life-giving warmth. Sarai squeezed her eyes shut, released her breath and felt the sunlight innervate her, warming her to the core. She knew the light of the sun and then *knew* All One came through the sun, rushing through the heavens, finding Its home within her. The One was all around her, warming her through and gently settling deep within her inner waters, where It touched a small, new life. A new voice whispered to her, calling her *Mother.* The child *called* to *Father.* Z'Shar smiled into Sarai's eyes, then stooped low to lay his ear to her belly. The three of them breathed together as One.

Nobody around them noticed their joy for the people stood silently, many with eyes closed against the bright sunlight, feeling the long-awaited warmth. But they were not long quiet. Soon they were laughing and talking to each other and even to the sun above. Suddenly, a rush of wind blew their hair away from their faces and six black-clad giants stood in their midst. The smaller people laughed, clapped their hands and shouted joyous greetings, crying happy tears. "She is here! She is here!" they called to each other and into the cavern recesses, from where more people came running towards the sunlight.

One of the newly appeared giants was a lithe, black-haired, beautiful woman. She had the same luminous black eyes as Z'Shar. As she met her son's eyes she moved nimbly in his direction, even as laughing people clasped her hands and hugged her waist. Her radiant smile reflected the joy in his face. For a moment, her glowing eyes looked into Sarai's face, *greeting* her.

A new peace followed the *greeting* into the Earth woman's heart. *You know me!*

Yes. And we will know each other more.

Z'Shar and his mother embraced for a long time, *sharing* all that had passed while they had been apart. Sarai easily *listened,* then tried to stop, thinking she was invading their boundaries. Z'Shar laughed and reached for her hand, drawing her closer and encouraging her to *listen. When you are like us there are no boundaries, unless you will it as I have taught you. We know each other much faster. I am hearing of many changes and it is important that you learn about them.*

Sarai's eyes glowed with the wondrous things she learned. When they had finished, the three released each other and stepped back. Sarai knew now that the woman's name was Sholan, though the mountain people simply called her Mother. Sholan turned and knelt down to be closer to the smaller people who reached for her, crowding around her like excited children. Out loud, she greeted them in their language. Her voice was low and reedy, like a bird's. The people clasped her fingers and told her all about their lives as fast as they could get the words out.

Sarai thought they were indeed like children with the beloved mother they had not seen in many moons. Sholan learned who had mated, who had welcomed children into the world, who had lost loved ones, who missed the land outside the cavern (everyone), who had made something with his hands and who had helped the sick.

Z'Shar put his arm around Sarai and moved her towards the five other newcomers, one woman and four men, who stayed slightly apart from the group. One or two mountain people addressed them, welcoming those who had come with Mother. The giants nodded and smiled, but did not speak, for they had not learned the tongue of the Earth people. Z'Shar stepped up to them, *calling* them to stand close together with him and Sarai. As he *spoke* inside with them, he also spoke aloud in the tongue of the mountain people. Shyly, Sarai followed his lead. She gained easy confidence, for the visitors were open and quick to *touch* her thoughts and *share* their own. They learned quickly and eagerly began to speak the new language.

After a short while, when Z'Shar felt the newcomers were sufficiently comfortable with the new words on their tongues and the new sounds in their ears, he beckoned them and the rest of the group into the cavern. "Let's go inside where it is warmer, for we have much to share with the entire community. Onog, Thora, some of you, please gather everyone and tell them to come to the eating place. We have much news to share. We will soon be able to leave the cavern!"

This was met with surprised cheers and abundant laughter as people hurried to accompany the giants into their cavern haven and to alert those who were still sleeping and did not know that the sun had arrived. While the storms kept darkness over the land, many people had slept long, well into the grayish days. Since Shanga was heavy with child, she and Ariza also spent long nights in their alcove.

Sarai *listened* for Grandfather Mendano and went to rouse him from his night's sleep. Arriving at his alcove, she found him just waking up. Excited words tumbled from her lips as she told the sleepy man about the newly arrived sunlight, the six giant visitors and the welcome news that they could leave the cavern to live under the sun once again. Grandfather was soon wide awake and throwing two warm furs around his tall frame. Grasping his granddaughter's hand he insisted on first running into the sunlight, where he drew in a deep breath of sweet, sun-touched mountain air. Then he turned and hurried back with Sarai to join the big gathering just outside his alcove.

TWENTY-THREE

GENESIS, IX

*1 And God blessed Noah and his sons and said unto them,
Be fruitful and multiply and replenish the earth.*

Sarai and Mendano pushed their way towards Z'Shar, who stood talking with the new Listeners at the center of the group. When all who dwelt in the great cavern had gathered in the eating space, the rock walls reverberated with laughter and excitement. Sholan waved her long arms above her head, trying to gather everyone's attention; as she was most familiar with the Earth people and their language, she would be the spokesperson for the visiting giants. Once most of the talking had died away, she raised her voice and spoke.

"When our sky ship came close to Earth, we saw the waters had covered most of the land. But now the sun is beginning to dry the waters and warm the land. We saw there are still people living in lands where the Earth is dryer and warmer than here in these mountains. We will take you wherever you choose so you can join the people there and live with them. The other giant men have not returned to the Earth, so they will not stop us as they might have before the Great Flood. You will be warm and you can find plenty to eat."

"Z'Shar told us there were places not covered by snows or water!" a man called out. Like Mar, his black hair fell to his waist.

"Yes, indeed there are, although they are far, far from here and you cannot walk there."

A small boy near her jumped up and down, pausing long enough to ask, "Will you really take us there in your sky boats?"

"Yes, we really will." Sholan smiled and reached out. "Come child, let me hold you." Grinning broadly, the child ran to her. She lifted him and held him gently on her hip. The boy's mother affectionately grasped her other hand.

Seeing this, three more small children approached the other visitors. One reached up towards the other giant woman and the others extended their arms towards two men. Their hands seemed to say, "Hold me close to you." The giants understood and lifted the children to their shoulders. Looking down on the crowd, the little ones beamed their delight.

Z'Shar said, "We will use my sky boat and also the one our visitors arrived in."

A thin woman addressed the giants. "And you? Will you stay with us?"

Mother shook her head, but she smiled. "We cannot stay, but

we will visit you on Earth often. Even after your children's children and their children are born, we will visit you. But we have a new home and we must return there. There is much work to be done."

"A new home?" echoed several voices.

"Yes, on a New World," Sholan explained. "You know we are from Home World, next to one of the stars in the skies. But the people on Home World are afraid of those of us who are Listeners. They hate us and decided to make us leave, banished us to another world."

Voices clamored and hummed in response.

Although he had already learned of these events, Z'Shar still did not completely believe they had come to pass. "Then all Listeners have been expelled from Home World?" he asked.

Their voices lost in the din, the six other aliens nodded. Though the excited voices in the cavern again began to quiet, the visitors chose to let their *words* share more detail with him.

"They said you have to go live in the sky?" called out a confused woman.

"They shouldn't hate you," said the child on Sholan's hip, angry at the giants far away. "That's mean. They are jealous because you can hear what they think."

"Oh, I think so too." Sholan nodded. "But I think they are also afraid of us. They found a place far away from Home World so they don't have to see us. And no, we don't have to live in the sky, but we must go to a new world, like the Earth, that is mostly covered by oceans. There is very little dry land and we must learn to live in this new world. We must learn to live in the water, too. And we have come to ask for your help."

"But how can we help you?" Shanga spoke up from the middle of the crowd.

Smiling, Sholan rested her eyes on Shanga's fertile belly. With one arm, she hugged the little boy on her hip and he giggled. She turned her eyes to the rest of the assembled people and explained, "Some of the things I must say to you are difficult for me—for us. We are ashamed and sad that our people have come and polluted your Earth. We have taken your riches and left behind what we have no more use for. Just by coming to Earth we have changed the people who live here. We have even put our seed into the daughters of the Earth.

"At the same time, we have joined with you; we are now part of each other. There will always be strong bonds between us. Some of you here are part giant, as you call us. Our blood, the blood of those from Home World, runs through you. And you are also strong and fertile for you were born on the Earth. You are a brave young people, able to survive in rough lands like this cold mountain land. You know how to find food anywhere you live. You can teach us much about surviving in a strange, new world.

"There are many more Listeners on the water planet waiting for us to return. We ask your help. Share with us what makes you strong. We invite you to come with us to our new ocean home. We know the people of Earth need you too and that you look forward to new homes outside this cavern. There is much to do after the Great Flood. We will take you wherever you choose to live on Earth—Earth is your home. But we also offer you a new home, a home among Listeners. The choice is yours."

Sholan drew a breath and rested. When she gently set the little boy on the ground, his mother took his hand and led him to his father and brothers. Other giants holding children stooped to lower them to the ground where the little ones slid down and scurried away to join their families. The visiting Listeners stood patiently, waiting while the people of the cavern talked excitedly among themselves. People laughed and cried in their happiness. They could leave the cold mountain land and live among other people in warmer lands! They had scarcely dreamed of this. The great cavern was filled with shouts and laughter.

Sarai *spoke* rapidly with Z'Shar. *Now, my beloved, you will never have to hide from the others again. You can live with your own people.*

You too, he was quick to remind her, *and our child. It is a strange new world, but we will be together and we will all help each other.*

I'm afraid, she owned. *I cannot fathom going far into the vast heavens in a sky chariot to a different—Earth.*

He *understood. I think not many people of the Earth will choose to fly far off into the vast blackness of an endless night. It is beyond their understanding and too frightening. But you and I have strength in our bonding and you need not fear. When I brought you here, you trusted me to support you in the strange flying over the land.*

And I trust you again, always.

Z'Shar knew the mountain-dwellers well. Most decided to stay on Earth, thrilled to be leaving the cavern the giants had made and the hard life of the high valley. They were eager to share their lives with the people who lived in the warmer lands far away. But that was as far as they wished to go. Leaving Earth made no sense to them; it frightened them.

From the middle of the group, near where Ariza and Shanga stood, Roe called out loudly so everyone would hear her words. "When he returned to us, Z'Shar told me the people in the village of my birth were above the flooding. I want to return home and take my grandmother's place as counselor to the people, as she wished me to."

Mar said, "Crue and I choose to go with Roe and live with her people. Earth is our home."

Roe grasped the hands of her tall, lean mate and young son. "My people live high in the far-away mountains where it is cold like here," she continued. "But we welcome anyone who wants to come with us. We will love and care for you, just as you did for me when I came to live with you."

Four families, coming through the crowd from different directions, were eager to go with Mar and Roe and join the new village. They hugged them and asked many questions about Roe's people and the land in which they lived. But most people talked enthusiastically about going to live where it was warm and food was easy to find.

The giants who had used this small community long ago had indeed spread their seed. Although only Mar was a Listener, it was easy to see that the blood of the giants was in many of the people. Mar's two younger cousins, Lan and Jad, were not yet mated. They were not as tall as Mar, but they stood a good head above most of the others. These two strong men stepped forward to the visitors, clasped hands with two giant men and pledged to accompany them to the new, ocean-covered world. Their commitments made, the two men of Earth plied the giants with questions and kept them busy long into the afternoon. The four soon moved to the cavern entrance so they could enjoy the bright sun while they talked.

Shanga and Ariza approached Mother and each grasped one of her hands. Ariza smiled at his mate. He nodded to her, encouraging her to speak.

"Mother," said Shanga solemnly, "I—I am afraid to travel so far away in a strange sky boat. But I can *hear* my daughter and I want her to live among Listeners. I know that I will be safe with Ariza and with you and Z'Shar and Sarai."

"I am happy you choose to join us. We need your help, your strength. And we will take care of you," Mother promised. "We will be your family too. I could tell you now that there is nothing for you to fear, but you will learn that for yourself."

"I *hear* my child," Shanga confided. "She is happy to be with Listeners."

"As I am," murmured Ariza. He let go of Sholan and hugged his mate.

Grandfather stood between Sarai and Z'Shar, an arm about each. When Shanga and Ariza had finished speaking to Sholan, he stepped forward and addressed her.

"I know my granddaughter will go with you," he said. "She and Z'Shar are my only family now. Will there be enough land to support all of you and your children and their children?"

"Yes," Mother replied. "My people are much older than the people of Earth. We do not have many children, but they all live long lives. There will always be a place for each of us."

Grandfather nodded his approval. "Now tell me," he continued. "Is this place—this water world—warm?"

Sholan smiled broadly, for she could also *hear* his thoughts. "Yes, it is very warm. Warm and comfortable. You can rest well there."

"Then I choose to go there with you and my family," he announced emphatically. "I have lived too many years already. I have lived far longer than a man of the Earth should live. I want to end my days where I am warm. I'll be happy with you."

Still holding Shanga, Ariza grinned broadly, his teeth flashing. "And now I know for certain I have made the right choice," he said. "I too will be warm again."

Sarai was not surprised by Grandfather's decision. Even so, she felt overjoyed and hugged him tightly.

TWENTY-FOUR

The Listeners' sky chariot was even more of an alien world to her than Z'Shar's smaller chariot. Closing her eyes, Sarai leaned back in the strange, metallic chair that was softer than a sleeping pallet. She was tired, felt herself heavy with her growing child, her son, though her flat belly told no one he was there. She imagined floating on a cloud in the sky; she could sleep.

But she did not want to sleep yet. She sat up, amused that the warm back of the chair followed her, cushioning her like a firm pillow. She opened her eyes wide to take in all the sights outside the window of this small chamber in the huge sky chariot. Though small, the chamber was nearly as big as Z'Shar's entire chariot.

A short while earlier, Z'Shar had brought his sky chariot to the entrance of the cavern, near where food was stored. As if held by invisible ropes, the bright round chariot hung in the cold morning air, just touching the wet earth. Their feet warm in their tall black boots, Sarai and Shanga walked through the mud and stepped into the alien craft. Like excited children, their eyes widened to take in all the strange sights: the bright coals that gave off no heat, smooth metal chairs and table, and the wide open window through which they could see the mountains and the sky all around them. Z'Shar had directed them to sit in the two chairs. He remained standing as he guided his chariot high above the mountain tops to join the Listener's chariot.

It had hung in the sky like a huge, hard-scaled dragon looking down upon the mountains as it hunted its prey. Hidden inside the smaller metal creature, Z'Shar and the two women had snuck up on the dragon and pierced its belly. Once inside the metal beast, the outside world had disappeared. Z'Shar led them out of his chariot into a chamber that resembled a high, smooth cavern. The walls, the floor, the ceiling—all were smooth, hard, gleaming and gray. They had walked through a narrow passage until they came to this smaller chamber.

Sarai looked at Shanga, squirming in the chair next to hers.

Shanga sighed. "This—sitting thing—is comfortable." She frowned. "But I don't want it to be. It is—wrong. I'm afraid everything will be strange from now on. What do you think?"

Sarai smiled and looked at the rest of the chairs around them. They were all identical and though she felt like she was resting on a cloud, she still expected the warm chair to be as hard and cold as the blade of a knife. "I can tell you this," she said slowly. "I have ridden before in Z'Shar's sky chariot. This one is much bigger. I can hardly believe my eyes when I see his chariot resting inside this giant chariot. But Shanga, this time I am not frightened like I was when Z'Shar brought me to our cavern. It is not so strange. I think we will get used to these things."

157

"I will have to get used to everything," sighed Shanga.

"We will all be together," said Sarai. She gazed at Shanga's swollen belly. "I hope your child will be born into the sun."

"Mother says it will be many days before we get home to our New Earth. That is so hard for me to understand. And all of our people gathered up everything and went to new places far away in just two days... I wish—I wish I had seen the lands where they went."

"Z'Shar, Ariza and the others are concerned that we are with child. They want us to stay safe."

Shanga sniffed. "Hmph. Pregnant women don't need to be secluded."

"I don't understand everything." Sarai shook her head. "But when I was a priestess in the Temple, if one of us got with child from one of the Gods—the giants—the child almost always died before it was born. And the few who survived to be born—well, they were sickly and weak and died in just a few months. We don't know how it will be for us. We need plenty of rest. I tire easily now, as you do."

"Yes, but Sarai, you are more giant Listener than you are woman of Earth... And both Ariza and I are of the Earth, even though Ariza has the blood of the giants. Surely we are not so weak."

"I suppose not, but I trust Z'Shar and Mother and I feel it is right to be safe."

Shanga sighed and shrugged her shoulders. "Oh, I have to agree. But I don't want to. It's like this thing I sit on—feels wrong, even though it's—I'm scared to go far away! I want to go, but I'm still scared."

Sarai nodded. "It's all right to feel scared. I think that will pass."

"Ariza isn't at all scared," Shanga mused. "He is so excited, so happy to go far away."

"We are all different," said Sarai thoughtfully. She squinted to look through the large window, larger than the one in Z'Shar's chariot although not so large as the huge window in the cavern wall. "They must be almost finished taking things from the cavern."

"Look there." Shanga pointed. "I see Z'Shar's sky boat. They're coming."

"I see it, too."

Gazing through the window, they watched the round, shining chariot rise above the mountains and move toward them. Sarai imagined the dragon chariot awaiting the arrival of its smaller servant. The approaching chariot disappeared beneath the larger Listeners' chariot.

Soon the four men born on the Earth—Grandfather, Lan, Jad and Ariza—tramped through the doorway into the sitting chamber, joking and laughing. Grandfather took a big bite of the red apple he held. Eyes lit with enjoyment, he swallowed the fruit and made his way to Sarai. Bending down, he kissed her cheek. She looked at him and he answered the questions in her eyes.

"All the fires have been put out—every last one of them. I never thought there were so many fires in the cavern, but I'm glad there were. It's really cold in there now." He shivered. "But not in here. Yes, it is good to feel warm." He pulled his fur tighter around his black shirt and pants.

Sarai felt suddenly hungry. "Are we bringing the rest of the food? And can I have a bite of that apple?"

He handed her the apple. "We have lots more," he said. "Just wait until you see the storage place on this—sky boat!" He laughed. "Yes, we brought everything with us, even some food the others brought from the faraway lands. Z'Shar said we would want it. Food will be—different on New Earth." He shook his head. "Thinking about that makes me feel kind of sick. Are we going to eat bugs or rocks or what?"

"I think we will like the food, but not as much as here," said Sarai, chewing. "That's what I *hear* from Mother and the others. They like Earth's food better."

"Hmm… Not sure I find that comforting. Well," he continued, "we also brought the rest of our furs. We don't have to wear them, but we can sleep on them. I'll like that."

Ariza eased himself into a metal chair next to Shanga. "I miss Crue and Roe and Mar," he said. They all nodded and Lan added, "I miss all our people."

"We will come back here often, just as Mother said," Grandfather reminded him. "I wonder, though. When I get warm, I may not want to leave New Earth."

"I wish we were there already," said Shanga. She rubbed her hands over her swollen belly. "She wants to come into the sun soon. I hope she waits until we get—home. I don't want her to be born on this sky boat. I want her to feel the sun and drink water from the world around us." Ariza kissed her cheek and slid a reassuring arm around her shoulders.

Z'Shar entered the chamber, arms loaded with several food and water containers that Sarai remembered from the day he had brought her to the cavern. She went to him as he deposited the containers into an empty metal chair. They hugged, warm together.

Still holding her, Z'Shar addressed the other Earth people. "As I told you before, we must destroy the cavern before we leave. It is not natural to the Earth. Also, we can leave no trace that we have been here. If the other giants choose to return—and I believe they will—they must never know that we have been here and taken all the people away." He paused as heads nodded in the little group, understanding. "Earth and this cavern have been home to me, too. I have chosen to watch here with you, the children of Earth. We will use light beams from our ship to end the cavern and restore the mountain."

Then the seven waited, suspended high above the mountains in the Listeners' great sky chariot. Sarai followed Z'Shar closer to the large window and stood with him, arms still around each other. She shivered, crying inside. Though she understood the cavern was not really of their Earth, she mourned its passing.

There was a familiar humming and the floor seemed to vibrate beneath her. A huge beam of light, white-hot and burning into her eyes, sprang from the sky ship and struck the mountain, glinting off the huge window before which she had stood only yesterday. Behind her somebody gasped, somebody shouted, somebody held his breath. Grandfather stepped beside her; she felt the warmth from his flesh. She reached for Mendano's hand and grasped it firmly. She moaned.

The light pierced deep within the mountain, as though it came from some huge fire-stick of the Gods. It sliced powerfully through

161

the mountaintop, shaking it to its core and melting the great, wide window and surrounding rocks. As she listened to the crashing, rumbling tumult of the collapsing cave, Sarai's heart quickened. Tears filled her eyes. For many of the people, the great cavern had been a prison from the open air; for others, simply a safe haven from the freezing, killing cold. But for Sarai, the cavern was her first home—the strange, safe place where she had found her people and learned to love freely. There she had bonded with Z'Shar and together they gave life to their child, their son. There she had first felt Spirit, the miracle of Life that holds us all in Her womb and courses through our veins.

Sadly, her mouth open, she watched her cavern home collapse and melt away. The mountain caved in on itself, as if the waters below had sucked it down to the valley floor. It reminded her of the time she had dug a hole in the wet sand at the beach. Seawater had seeped through the ground, filling the hole, while gentle waves rippled forward to cover it. When the waters retreated, the sand was smooth and flat, as if she had never dug the hole.

The humming ceased; the light beam disappeared. Hundreds of massive boulders rolled and crashed down the sides of the mountain to be swallowed up by the dark waters below. The tallest and most majestic of the mountain family was gone, leaving only a humble brother to huddle among his taller siblings.

Silence followed, as if they all held their breath in a prayer for the dead cavern. Gently, Z'Shar released Sarai and, taking Grand-father by the hand, led him to a warm, comforting chair. Mendano eased into the seat and closed his eyes. "I'm weary," he said.

"This is something you never dreamed you would see," said Z'Shar. "Maybe it is too much right now. Sleep. All of you." He raised his eyes to the others. "Sleep and be comforted. You will not know fear. You are safe here."

Shanga, Lan and Jad smiled and nodded, closing their eyes. But Ariza stood and said, "I want to see everything that happens. I am not afraid to feel these things."

Z'Shar nodded and reached out to him, beckoning him to follow. Sarai also walked to his side.

"You and the child should rest," he told her.

"Not yet," she said. "Soon. I will come here and sleep next to Grandfather. I, too, wish to see us leave the Earth behind."

"I want to be awake as long as I can," said Ariza, raising his hands. "I relish the new. I am not tired."

"I think even you will want to sleep before too long," said Z'Shar, and he grinned. "But I am glad you want to share with us. Come, both of you, to the main chamber, where we guide the ship to our destination."

Sarai glanced back at the other people from Earth who were already asleep, worn out from witnessing the miraculous devastation. Then she and Ariza accompanied Z'Shar into the sky ship's corridors.

TWENTY-FIVE

As she and Ariza followed Z'Shar through the corridors of the sky ship, Sarai stared at the smooth metal walls. She reached out with inquisitive fingers, letting them slide along the walls as she walked. Everywhere in the alien ship she saw hard metal, the stuff of knives and swords. Like the Gods' fire-sticks. The "gods" who were not gods had wielded nearly absolute power over the people of Earth. How strange it was that this same metal housed and protected the kind Listeners who knew the All One…

They reached a large, circular chamber where they found Mother and the other Listeners who had come to Earth. The great Guiding Chamber was larger than the whole of Z'Shar's traveling chariot, but looked similar to it. There were many more strange yet comfortable metal chairs where people sat, their hands busy on the nearby tables with the bright colored coals that gave off no heat. Sarai swayed as she heard the now familiar humming that signaled the chariot's departure. Clasping a hand of each, Z'Shar hurriedly pulled Sarai and Ariza to the three closest chairs. Each nestled into his or her chair. *How strange,* thought Sarai again, *to settle into this metal as if it was a pillow.* There was some pressure above her heart and belly, as she remembered from riding in Z'Shar's chariot. *Nothing to fear.* The humming grew louder until it filled her ears. Invisible giant hands seemed to press her into the chair and then release her as the humming dwindled into the background. She let out her breath and wriggled her toes. *I wonder when we can get up and walk around again?*

Soon, Z'Shar reassured her and then nodded to Ariza who, Sarai realized, had asked the same question.

When Sarai noticed Mother and others leave their chairs, she tentatively sat forward. She grimaced then giggled as the alien chair seemed to follow her body, helping her. Planting her feet on the floor, she raised her eyes to look out the large window before her and caught her breath.

A huge, shining sky chariot loomed before them, filling the entire Guiding Chamber window. Brilliant fires flared near the chariot's base and now that Sarai could no longer hear the humming from the Listeners' sky chariot she heard—or felt—thundering from the giant ship outside. Suddenly their window to the skies was filled with the sight of a great inner chamber. Sarai saw a huge, circular room that looked like their Guiding Chamber, filled with many giant men. Her heart thudded against her breast as she recognized some of them, including their leader, who spoke. When she closed her eyes, it was as if A–Don's harsh voice boomed into his metal speaking cup and she trembled as she had when a small child.

"You mutants are not allowed here!" he shouted. "We know you have some of the Earth people with you." His eyes narrowed and seemed to thrust into her like sharp daggers. "Sarai," he hissed, "you do not belong here. Nor do the others," he continued, his voice escalating. "Return them whence they came! They are contaminants and must not leave the Earth lest they pollute our Home World."

Sholan spoke calmly, without fear. "We are not your slaves to command. All Listeners have been expelled from your Home World and we live on a new Home World. The people of Earth who have chosen to come with us are descended from your Home World as much as from Earth. It is you who have polluted the people of the Earth. They belong with us."

"Mutant woman, you will obey me!" A-Don commanded, his face flushed.

How well Sarai recognized him! He could not understand anyone defying him. With a will of their own Sarai's eyes scanned him, taking in the red flames of his hair and beard, the ruddy pink skin, narrow blue eyes and massive chest. Her belly roiled as she remembered the strong odor of him when he was on top of her, thrusting himself inside her. Bitter juices rose in her throat. She *knew* where he was weak in his manly parts. They could hurt him, destroy him! Her breath fluttering, she *sent* what she *knew* to Z'Shar and Sholan.

Sholan *replied, No need to hurt him. We know where they are all weak. There are many ways to overcome these people. They cannot harm us. Join with us now. Together we will stop them and they will let us pass.*

Sarai held her breath, afraid to believe the gentle woman. She and the people of the city had always been powerless against the giant men. They had done what they pleased with the people of Earth and struck down any who opposed them. Not so long ago, they had killed everyone she loved and she hated them.

Remember, Z'Shar's *voice* came to her, *they are also your people. But they cannot hear you as you hear them. They cannot touch you; they cannot harm us. So we do not harm them. We leave them. Come, Sarai, do not be afraid. Join with us now. We listen together as one. Feel all of us—Ariza is here too, joined. He is ready. Open, Sarai. Make yourself open and ready.*

Still Sarai hesitated. How could she forget how these cruel men had hurt and killed so many of her people? She wanted them to suffer for what they had done.

No, said Z'Shar. *Do not hate them. When you hate them, you give them power. You become more like them. They can no longer hurt you or the ones you love. Leave them. Let them go.*

Sudden understanding burst through her in a huge wave. Grateful tears cascaded down her cheeks. *I am not like them!* she *shouted.* No, she was not like her cruel Masters of yore. She was whole and she was safe. Her fears left her, flew out the window to be lost forever in the vast blackness. The giant "gods" would never touch her again. She chose to let them go.

Now, join with us, all the Listeners *called* to her with one *voice. We tell them to go away.*

Go away, Sarai *said* with them, all as one.

A-Don and the other giants disappeared from the window, which was again filled with their enormous sky ship. The Listeners watched the fires flare and grow brighter at the base of the other ship. They felt the thundering rumble through their bones as the ship backed away until they saw no more of it. Only blackness, studded with tiny lights and the blue oceans of Earth below filled the window.

Ariza rose from his chair and jumped up and down. The encounter with the false gods had exhilarated him. He was Ariza the brave, who loved whatever was new and different. He was excited to live it all.

But Sarai gasped and shuddered. A piece of her had died and though she was glad to lay that part to rest, she was exhausted. Conflicting feelings swam about and tangled up like seaweed within her. Most of her life she had been powerless against the giant Gods. She had always wished them death and suffering when she saw them hurt the people of Earth. Not long ago she had triumphantly killed one and raged that she could not kill others. Then she learned they were in her blood and she was ashamed to be one of them until she found herself, became all she was. Today they had sought to dominate her and her family again. But the Listeners were One and the giants were powerless against them. She let them all go.

Finally, the woman who was both of the Earth and of the skies wanted only to sleep. She did not remember when Z'Shar took her hand and led her back to the chamber where the other people of Earth were sleeping. He guided her to the welcoming chair next to Grandfather, who snored gently. The soft, warm chair cradled her and sleep beckoned. Z'Shar stood next to her, holding her hand, stroking her hair. She surrendered to sweet, loving rest.

EPILOGUE

She opened her eyes to bright light. The salty smell of the sea tickled her nostrils and she heard water lapping at the beach. She looked into Z'Shar's smiling eyes. Cradling her in his arms, he carried her over the sands. As she gazed through the warm mist above, she saw two small yellow-white suns circling each other, dancing in a deep blue sky.

She was naked, as was Z'Shar; he must have removed her black clothing before carrying her outside the great chariot. Looking deeply into her mate's dark eyes, Sarai *joined* with his *hearing*. Their child awoke within her and *listened* to them.

Z'Shar stopped and leaned forward, gently releasing her. Sarai stretched her bare feet to the ground and stood beside him, wriggling her toes in the deliciously warm sand. She turned around several times, soaking in the ethereal sights of the long, sparkling beach and the shimmering blue waters, a blue as vibrant as a peacock's feather. Everywhere she looked were willowy trees laden with long strings of blue-green leaves that swayed with the breeze. Many of the trees were tall, but others barely reached above her head. Some were rooted in the sand near the water and there were even a few large trees with massive, dark brown trunks in the distance, rising out of the sea. But most grew out of the turquoise thickets bordering the sands. Naked, brown-skinned Listeners wandered by the lush bushes, pulling off red and purple berries, talking and laughing with each other as they ate their fill.

Everyone was here, her family from Earth and the Listeners who had brought them in their sky chariot. Many other Listeners, who had stayed behind, greeted the travelers and welcomed the children of Earth to their new Home World. She saw Ariza tug at Shanga's arm, wanting her to go into the sea with him. His mate smiled and shook her head, her long black hair glinting in the sunshine. He smiled, nodded and kissed her mouth before releasing her arm. Turning on his heel, he ran into the vibrant blue waters and dove beneath. Moments later, he burst through the surface and laughed up at the bright suns.

Shanga still wore her black pants that stretched around her full, round belly. Carefully, she stooped and sat on the golden-white sand. She smiled and wrapped her arms around her front, hugging the child within. Yes, her daughter had waited until they reached their New Earth—she would be born under the two small suns.

Sarai *heard* her *calling, Sarai, I can hear you! My child has shown me how.* Without words or touch, the two women embraced. Warm in this love, Sarai *heard* Grandfather Mendano. Z'Shar put his arm about her and pointed to the white-bearded man standing off to one side, farther from the water. Alone among the people on the beach, Grandfather still wore his black shirt and pants, although he had relinquished the two furs he had worn on top of his clothing. He bent down and went to the sand on his hands and knees, sifting the shimmering grains through his fingers and grinning as he drew in their heat. Slowly, sensuously, he turned around again and again in the sand, dragging his bare feet so that they drew a circle around him. Sarai *called* to him, but he did not *hear*. It did not matter. She knew he was happy in his warm sand circle.

She turned to the sea. Z'Shar dropped his arm from her shoulders, bent to kiss her cheek and then stepped back. Sarai walked a few steps and waded into the water until it caressed her knees. She was surprised how warm it was: not as hot as bath water but comfortable, as though it had been next to her flesh for a good while. She stooped, cupped some in her hands and brought the seawater to her lips. It was warm and salty on her tongue, like her tears.

Distant chattering caught her ear. Glancing out to sea, she spied gray-blue dolphins leaping out of the water. *Have the dolphins also come from Earth? Or were they already living here in the sea?*

They were always here, said Z'Shar.

Wading further into the water, she squeezed her eyelids shut as the water covered her head. She remembered another time she had walked into the water, not so long ago, in a colder sea she had loved on Earth. *Good-bye, Earth.*

She let the salt water buoy up her legs until she floated on her back. Welcoming her, the warm sea held her in its arms and soothed the aches of the long, strange journey. When she opened her eyes, she saw the twin suns dancing above. Soon she would hug Grandfather as he reveled in the suns' heat. Closing her eyes once more, she *called* to Z'Shar and the others and they *answered*. Rocked gently at the edge of the vast blue sea, she was One with All. Home.

ACKNOWLEDGMENTS

Many thanks to my fellow writers—Jean, Dan, Linnea, Brian, Dorothy, Cynthia, Joe, Doug, Dick, Craig, Laurie and Diane—for their feedback, suggestions and (most of all) encouragement.

Hugs and thanks to my Brother Bob. You were my first reader and helped me get to this place.

To Diane, my Spiritual Sister on our great journey: I know you're with me at every turn in the road. You helped bring *Seed of the Gods* from inside me out to the written pages. Thank you.

To Tom—Thanks for loving the real me so I could write this book. I am always grateful for your knowledge and support as I confront computers and technology on my 21st century author's quest.

I got the idea for this story when I was reading the Bible.

Made in the USA
San Bernardino, CA
13 September 2016